CN00879750

MY EROTICA
OUT TO DRY

Mister Average

DEDICATION

This work is dedicated to all those who have sexual fantasies.

ACKNOWLEDGEMENTS

Cover image licensed by Depositphotos.com/ColorValley

This is a work of fiction. All the characters are fictitious.

Author's note: All characters depicted in this work of fiction are 18 years of age or older.

CONTENTS

1 INTRODUCTION

Hello, my name is Mister Average, and for the past three years I have been writing and publishing erotica under a number of different names.

I am quite a prolific short story writer, and have published nearly three million words, mostly erotica.

It is quite an interesting career - I guess it is my job to walk around thinking sex all the time and looking for sex based ideas and scenarios and then writing about it. I suppose researching sex, for me, is a tax deduction – that's funny, isn't it.

I enjoy writing erotica, it's mentally stimulating, but it is also rewarding because of the pleasure others get from my work.

I enjoy seeing a review where the reader has clearly enjoyed my work - that makes me feel appreciated.

I remember one reader declaring that 'The Girl Who Farted During Sex' was the funniest thing they had ever read. That inspires me to write more.

I enjoy knowing that the reader is stimulated, and that they might please themselves after reading my work. I sometimes wonder how many orgasms I have been responsible for!

I am not a famous or well-known erotica author, just one of the many plodding along out of the limelight waiting for that break that never comes.

Today I decided to take a day off from writing, and instead just put together a compilation of stories that have pleased me the most, and to share them with you in a single volume. I hope you enjoy them.

There is a varied selection here.

The Girl Who Farted During Sex is probably the funniest story I have written and gets good reviews, you have the human weakness stories like Punishing the Wife and Ghostwriter, there is the story of betrayal and counter betrayal in the Maid, I touch on cuckoldry in the Cuckold Husband in the Park and I have added two of my futurist erotica stories, Robo-Sex and the scary 23rd Century Sex. To cap it all off there is my little story called Heaven, which makes you wonder what choice you would make.

Oh, and whilst I have your attention, just a little friendly word to those who leave reviews stating that a story is too short. If you buy something which clearly states it is a short story, and short stories are usually under about 8,000 words, there is no point complaining the story is too short.

Short stories are exactly that – fast paced and to the point, no time to breathe!

I hope you all enjoy my work, I write for your sexual and emotional pleasure.

2 PUNISHING THE WIFE

Steve was away for the weekend, with some work colleagues, and eager to get up to no good, but after his friends ran off with college girls he was left alone in the bar - until Carla turned up. Steve immediately wanted the older woman, he followed her to Carla's hotel room and enjoyed himself - until Carla's husband entered the room and caught them at it, and punished them.

Steve didn't mind having a drink with friends when he was out on the town and interstate. He had planned this for some time so that two of his colleagues would also be in town over that weekend and they could get up to a bit of fun whilst they were away from wives or girlfriends.

Funny how you always plan these things to go a certain way, but in reality they just don't end up like that, and rarely is a night out as exciting as you had hoped it would be.

He was out of town, footloose and fancy free and he was after some nice and new pussy - and to hell with his wife, grumpy bitch!

In fact, he hoped he would get a chance to bone some slut tonight and he hoped she was married to some loser. He liked that idea - fuck the woman and send her home to her husband with a pussy full of his muck. Steve smiled and drained his drink and motioned to the barman to give him the same again. He had high hopes for the night.

Of course, to many of those looking at Steve on that night, it would have seemed as though he was the loser, but he didn't realize that.

The air of the hotel bar was filled with the sad attempt at piano music provided by a drunken old man sitting at the

9

piano in the corner. Steve looked at the guy as he continued nursing his drink; he was bored now, horny and bored.

He had joined two of his friends on what he thought would be a sensational weekend of booze and girls, they were all away from home and looking for sex.
But it hadn't worked out like that for Steve - instead his two friends had been swept away by two young and gorgeous college cheerleaders who, oh so conveniently, did not have a third friend. So Steve was left at the hotel bar, all alone and knocking back drink after drink.

He found his surroundings to be mind-numbingly boring and he was so pissed off he thought of going to bed soon. The few women who were scattered around the bar were either with someone, or he could easily see why they weren't - which was a bit uncharitable since he was no hot looker himself.

He figured after a few more drinks his mind might be dizzy enough to take anything with legs and breasts that walked through the door, that would do him just fine – at least he would get his dick into some wetness.
Steve was one of these guys who thought a bit of pussy was better than no pussy at all!

But instead what greeted his eager gaze was a sight he never expected and suddenly the evening changed for him.

CARLA

Her legs were long, and her breasts were full beneath the low cut collar of her burgundy dress. Its colour accented her skin tone which was pale and flawless. Her hair tumbled in loose chocolate curls that made him ache to run his fingers through it. She was older, but he was most impressed by the way she walked and how she carried herself with confidence and authority, this was a woman of style and breeding!

He watched her as she strode across the bar to a small table not far from him. She was instantly served her drink of choice. As she sipped it, she glanced in his direction. He thought it was his imagination, that she was gazing at him sexily while she took another swallow of her drink.
He told himself, as the heat rose in the base of his stomach, that she could have any man she laid her eyes on, yet she was looking at him.
Her eyes lingered on him, and he could feel them slowly surveying his physical prowess from his broad shoulders to the youthful curve of his ass on the bar stool.
Slowly, she stood from her chair. She picked up her drink and wandered toward the bar.

Steve could not believe his luck when she sat down beside him. He was too nervous to speak as she leaned across him to pick up his glass.
 She held it up to the bartender and pointed to her own, indicating that the young man should have what she was drinking.
Steve couldn't believe it; this was the material of dreams, not of any reality he had ever lived in.

"I thought you would like it, and by the way, I am Carla," she whispered just beside his ear. Steve could feel his heart pounding harder and his cock was starting to twitch in his pants.
This woman was hot and so confident, he wanted her badly!

She lifted her glass toward his lips, and he willingly took a sip. The liquid was strong and sweet, their eyes were locked onto each other's as Steve sipped the sweet nectar.

Her perfume wafted around him as she leaned just a little

closer, letting her breast's brush along his arm as she pretended to take a peek at his watch.

"Hmm, getting late, isn't it honey?" she murmured as the bartender set down Steve's drink. Steve could not take his eyes off of her as she downed her own drink, and waited expectantly for him to do the same. He did not hesitate. When the strong alcohol struck him it made him a little dizzy. The sensation mixed with the heat of his arousal led him into a heady place of pleasure. He ached to touch her, but he was not sure that he should, was she just a tease, or was she for real?

Carla stood from the bar and began to turn away, Steve's eyes following her every move. He reached up to grasp her hand, afraid to let her disappear, and she slid her room key into his palm. Without looking back she left the bar and took the elevator up to her room, Steve watched as her ass wiggled, inviting him to enjoy it.

It only took him a moment to get the message and jump up from the bar stool. He followed behind her and took the next elevator up to the floor designated on the room key. As he rode the elevator up to the floor he mused about this sudden change in fortune.
Fifteen minutes ago he had been feeling down and out, a weekend wasted, but here he was now heading for a rendezvous with a stunning older woman.

He considered her for a moment, she was very attractive, very confident, and probably in her fifties. He had never screwed a woman that old before, but he was sure she was very experienced and he would be treated to a lot of very hot sex.
His cock stirred again in his pants as the elevator door opened in front of him.

THE HUSBAND

It had been a long day for Angelo, his work in government security kept him away from home often. Today had been no different; he had been in the President's entourage as the head of state conducted the business of meeting's, pressing the flesh and more meetings. Angelo's day had started at 4am, in another city and he had worked until 5pm. Then it was a quick trip to the airport to catch the shuttle back home only to find a note from his wife saying she was having drinks with her girlfriend Sharon at a city hotel.

Angelo was no fool; he knew his attractive wife was a slut and that she took advantage of his absences. He kind of accepted it as one of the hazards of his important job that he was away from home, and his wife left to her own devices. Angelo knew there would be no Sharon and there would be no girl's night out.

Angelo knew his wife would be downtown in some posh bar looking for some younger man to fuck and he guessed she would be in the bar of one of a handful of hotels.

It didn't take long for Angelo to find his wife, he had rung the bars of a few hotels and on his third call the barman agreed that there was indeed a woman matching Angelo's description over the phone sitting in front of him at the bar. And when Angelo provided a secret service number the barman identified, discretely, the number of the room he was charging her drinks to.

Angelo hung up, reached for his coat, calmly, and drove to the city to deal with his hopeless wife.
His fingers tapped over the steering wheel as he imagined his wife on her knees being rammed from behind by some younger stud. He whistled softly as he imagined her sucking

on some other guy's dick. He had seen it all before, she just couldn't help herself. He blamed himself for not being the best of husband's because of his obsession with his job. He blamed himself for not being an overly exciting lover, and even though it was not his fault, he blamed himself for having a small dick.

As he pulled into the driveway of the hotel he wondered how different things would have been if he had one of those nice, big thick cocks you see in porn videos. It would have all been different then, he reasoned, she would have been begging him for it.

SEX!

When Steve found the right room he reached up to knock on the door, only to find it swung open beneath the pressure of his knuckles. The room was dark, and at first it was hard to see anything in the gloom. He took a few steps forward, dragging his feet so as to not trip over anything and look like a complete nutter. He imagined that she was inside the room somewhere, hopefully already naked in bed and waiting for him. As his eyes adjusted to the gloom he was able to make out more of the room and he could see the bed over in the far corner. He took a few steps closer towards the bed; he felt quite drunk and was as horny as hell. He hoped she was ready for a hammering because he was going to give it to the bitch!

Finally, as he closed in on the bed, he heard a voice call out softly, and seductively,

"Over here, lover."

He moved to the sound of her voice.
Through the shadows he could make out her naked figure stretched across the bed invitingly. She did not speak, she only gestured for him to join her on the bed. Steve did not

need any more encouragement. He walked over to join her and stood there next to the bed looking down at her; he pulled aside the covers and revealed her completely naked body.

She was stunning, especially for a woman her age. Steve quickly unbuttoned his shirt and then unzipped his pants and let them fall to the ground. The woman reached up with her hand and rubbed the rapidly swelling front of his underpants.

Steve moaned as she rubbed the fabric of his underwear against his cock and then gasped as her fingers quickly slipped under the elastic and she grabbed onto his dick. Steve loved it, and knew his cock would soon be standing hard and rigid.

The woman helped him out and pulled Steve's manhood out of his underpants. It sprang to attention and she stroked it lovingly a few times before getting on her knees and licking it.
Steve could see more clearly now, he watched as she peeled back the foreskin of his big dick and then ran her tongue over the exposed flesh. She was an amazing woman.

He watched as she eagerly took all of it into her mouth and sucked expertly, he couldn't remember being sucked like this before.
His wife was not a big fan of oral sex, this woman was the best! He savoured every moment of the oral treatment and felt a thrill of delight run through him.

As quickly as she had started she took his dick out of her mouth and looked up at him.

"Get your pants off and come to bed sweetie, we have business to conduct," she commanded as she smiled seductively at him.

Steve slipped his underpants off and threw off his shoes and socks and lay down next to her in the large bed.

As he lay there next to her he could feel their bare skin brushing against each other's. Steve began to speak, but Carla pressed her lips to his before he could.

"Shhh," she said, "let's just fuck, ok honey?"

Steve nodded his acceptance of her terms and lay back and waited for the sexual bliss that was promised.

Her fingertips wandered along his bare chest and stroked the firmness of his muscles. Steve coasted his palms down along her breasts and Carla gasped through their kiss as the warmth of his touch grazed across her hardening nipples.

She squirmed closer to him and slid one leg over his, drawing his solid cock closer to the heat of her pussy as she flexed her body against his. Steve groaned and broke away from her lips to taste her neck. When he felt the crack of her hand against his bare ass, he grinned and bit her tender flesh softly.

He caught a nipple between his teeth and flicked it lightly with his tongue as his hand rolled over her other breast. The fingers of his other hand were wandering across the slope of her stomach as she grasped his cock and stroked it eagerly. She sighed with pleasure and arched her back as he switched from breast to breast, sucking and nipping as he did.

Steve was an eager man; he was not going to be denied her sinful pleasures.

His fingers started to roam across her body, circling her belly button and then moving slowly over her little tufted mound. She kissed and sucked his mouth as she waited for him to touch her forbidden parts. When his fingers slid over her clit her whole body shuddered with desire. His fingers pulled lightly at her fleshy bud and he rolled it between his fingers, she groaned as the electric excitement ran through her body. He teased her and pulled her labia gently. He could tell from how moist she was that she was as turned on as he was. He crushed his lips back to hers and she shifted beneath him as she spread her legs open for him. He then slid his finger into her as he continued to toy with her clit and it entered into her very moist love hole.

She thrust her hips up against him as he hovered over her, and he took the movement as an invitation but he wasn't ready to fuck her yet, he wanted to taste the sweetness of her nectar first.
He raised himself and moved down towards her open slit. He ran his tongue lightly over it and she wrapped her thighs around his head, drawing him into her, preventing him from leaving her sweet muff.
He peeled her folds open with his fingers and licked her generously, tasting her cunt, smelling her sex scent and getting very aroused.
He knew his cock was ready to explode but he had a long way to go yet. As he feasted on her vulva he maneuvered his cock around towards her face, offering it to her for more sucking.
She took the hint and grabbed his rigid dick and lapped along the shaft, tasting him, and then swallowing his cock whole as she took him completely.
For an older woman she had a nice moist pussy, hairy, with swollen lips but a tight opening. As he licked her cunt he looked into it, and looked along to her anus, which his fingers were also holding open. He could smell the mustiness of her other forbidden hole, he wondered if she would let him use that tonight as well.

She was continuing to suck him hard and he was loving every minute of it. He was justifying his behaviour on the basis that his wife didn't suck cock and he needed it, desperately.

She was moaning onto his cock. She removed it for a moment and called out, "Mmm, oh yes, mmmm, I would like to feel your fingers in there."

Steve responded.

"Oooh yeh, put it inside," she said moaning as he entered her vagina with his thick digit.

As he worked on her, he could hear the squelching as his fingers moved around inside her.

"Oooh yeh," she continued, her body rising up to meet his hand, her hips moving to his rhythm.

"Ohh, it's so good, mmmm, I like it so much."

"Oohh yes, mmmm, baby," she whimpered as Steve treated her to his finger fucking.

He was fucking her mouth as he licked and fucked her vagina with his digits, but Carla soon took control, she knew what she needed and she was going to get it.

She spat out his cock and called out to Steve, " C'mon lover, I need that cock of yours inside my pussy."

Steve did as he was told and lifted himself up and knelt between Carla's legs. He looked down at her offered cunt and lowered himself, lining up his dick in his hand and guiding it into her swollen vaginal opening.

He pushed the head of his bulbous penis against the opening of her pussy and thrust deep inside of her. She felt so tight and wet; it was amazing feeling himself enter her body. She cried out and writhed under him as he continued to grind into her.

He watched as her tits floated and jiggled with his every thrust into her cunt. He rammed his dick in as far as it would go, he loved it. He just wanted to use her, this slutty older woman. He wondered about her husband and smiled inwardly, he was fucking the loser's wife.

The couple kissed and sucked each other's tongue as they fucked like wild animals. Carla had her legs wrapped around Steve, calling out to him, encouraging him, urging him on to fuck her harder and harder. Her body was bathed in sweat, her cunt gushing as he pounded her, she was screaming loudly.

"Fuck me, Steve, fuck me hard, god I need your cock inside me, god I want your cum inside me."

"Oh yes, oh yes, Carla, your cunt is so tight, let me fill you, I want to empty my balls inside you."

"Oh yes, screw me, pound me, I am your cum slut, fuck me hard!!"

Carla moaned and begged him for more as she grasped his hips and ass and rocked her hips up to meet his strokes. She gasped and shivered as she reached the edge of orgasm, and in the same moment Steve moaned into her neck as he thrust as hard and deep as he could, spilling all of his pent up desire inside of her.

"Oh yes, I am cumming," he bellowed and pumped her harder as he edged towards his cliff.

"Oh yes, oh yes!"

"Fill me Steve, do it, do it, fill me up, I want your cum."

"Ahhhhhhhhh," he cried as he released all of his sperm inside her, pumping it in great globs into her inviting vagina.

"Yes, yes,yes."

CAUGHT!

They were both too caught up in the euphoria of their pleasure to notice that the door to the hotel room had swung open again.

Angelo, Carla's husband, strode in quickly and walked towards the bed. He stood there at the foot of the bed looking down at the two. He watched as the two shared their orgasm, growing more furious with every grunt and moan.

As Steve began to roll away from her, Angelo reached down and grabbed the younger man by the back of his neck. Steve had no idea what had hit him, he was stunned.

"Angelo!" Carla exclaimed as Steve cursed and struggled to get free of the much larger man's grasp. Angelo shot a withering glare in Carla's direction.

"Be quiet, and wait your turn, you dirty, slutty bitch!" he yelled sternly to his wife as she sank back against the bed and blushed with shame. She looked down at her nudity, and covered her breasts with her arm.
She knew it was a pointless exercise, she knew her husband had seen everything; she knew her husband had seen Steve pump her full of his sperm. She knew what Angelo was like under these conditions, she shuddered.

"Who are you?" Steve asked as he tried to pry Angelo's big

hand off of his neck.

Angelo did not answer as he dragged Steve to the edge of the bed.

"Seriously, I had no idea she was with anyone, I swear, I didn't know she was married or anything, just let me go and I won't ever see her again," Steve insisted as he wondered what the man was planning.

When Angelo sat down on the edge of the bed and tossed Steve across his muscular legs, Steve was too stunned to speak.

It was not until Angelo's large hot hand slammed down across Steve's bare ass, that the younger man realized what was happening.

He let out a yelp of pain with the first strike and panicked, squirming against Angelo's lap as he tried to escape. Angelo held him firmly in place and swung his hand down again, and again, leaving many large red welts on Steve's pale skinned bottom.

Steve gasped and winced as the pain spread through him like hot pins. Never in his life had he imagined he would be tossed across another man's lap and spanked, but as the third and fourth strikes hit, the severity of the pain made him certain that this was real.

On the bed Carla was embarrassed that she had been caught, but watching Angelo spank Steve made her ache with desire, it was arousing her, she could feel the heat welling up inside her. She crept a little closer to the two on the bed, while Angelo was distracted with another spank across Steve's poor crimson ass.

"Please," Steve begged with a whimper.

"I swear, I didn't know she was married, just let me go. She wasn't even any good, she was just a cheap fuck, honest!"

Angelo was infuriating by Steve's absurd comments, he drew his arm back and then smacked him several times, punctuating each of the words he spoke.

"You will not fuck my wife you piece of scum, you will not ever touch her sacred body again, do you hear, shithead?"

He didn't receive a response and followed up with yet another sharp crack across the already bruised skin. When he realized Carla had sneaked up beside him, Angelo shoved Steve off of his lap and in the same swift movement he snatched her by her arms and dragged her across his knees. She could feel his hard cock through his pants as it pushed against her.

"I told you to wait your turn, slut." He admonished Carla and made his point with a vicious smack against her ass. Carla screamed and wriggled against him.

Steve stumbled to his feet and frantically searched for his clothes, while Carla received another swat across her backside.
She whimpered, but her pussy was dripping with arousal, and, of course, with Steve's semen dribbling out of her slit. Steve was just about to the door when he glanced back at the pair in time to see Angelo's hand falling against Carla's ass, leaving a bright red trail along her flesh.
Carla gazed up at Steve with a glaze of pleasure in her eyes, and Steve found himself intoxicated with desire.
He dropped his clothes back to the floor and seized his cock with his hand and started rubbing himself. He watched as Angelo continued to spank Carla, much to her pleasure.

The more she groaned with desire, the harder Angelo's strong hands struck her, until finally she began to whimper.

"Please, no more," She begged Angelo, which only made him swat her several more times.

"You do not fuck other men, do you hear, bitch? Do you hear me, are you listening to me, you dirty, cheap slut?" he asked sternly followed by a barrage of smacks.

With each smack of her flesh Steve continued to pull himself harder. He was moving closer to the couple and flogging his already used penis.
He was wild with excitement, he had never seen anything like this before, he had never seen someone being spanked, and he had never been smacked before.
Steve rubbed his swollen dick, and moaned and groaned, loudly enough for the other two to notice. They turned towards him, and Angelo laughed.

"Oh, you are as sick as us two, you dirty man. Go on do it again, blow your load all over the slut, blow it over her ass!"

Steve grew closer to his climax, his cock was ready, he had closed his eyes. When Angelo began rubbing and soothing Carla's ass, soothing the pain he had created, Steve cried out loudly and came onto Carla's ass.

Angelo glanced up sharply as he heard Steve groan with pleasure.
Before he could speak, Steve was on his knees beside him, his face upturned, and his breath heavy.
"Is it my turn again for being naughty?" He asked.

3 THE GHOSTWRITER

She had been his ghost writer for a few years, writing erotica. He would give her the ideas, she would fill in the blanks - it worked well. They had even met once and spent a weekend of uncontrolled passion. But now she was divorced, drinking too much and her writing was stale. As Erik abused her over the phone for non-delivery of work, she had an idea - and 30 minutes later they met in a hotel room.

For a few years they had been a successful team. He came up with the ideas and the passion, the excitement, the dirtiness, and she filled in the blanks. He told her who would be involved and what they would do; she would fill in the naughty details, the dialogue, and take the characters on the prearranged journey.

She was his ghost writer and they made a successful team. She could not write under her own name and lacked the imaginative ideas that Erik seemed able to come up with on a daily basis. She was good at filling in the story and writing the dialogue.

Indeed, they had become quite a prolific team, they didn't write best sellers but they churned out their short stories in copious quantities and they grew comfortable – and that was the problem.

They had forgotten what it was like to be risqué, to be naughty, to operate outside the square.

A few years earlier, when they had first started their writing relationship, they had both become excited over a few of their works and had exchanged emails, saucy emails, which had taken the relationship beyond a business relationship. It started with dirty messages to each other, and then they would deliberately write to excite each other, hoping the other would steal away and masturbate.

One day they finally moved to a face to face meeting and spent a weekend fucking each other's brains out and reliving the sordid acts of the characters in their books.

They experimented, pushed each other to sexual limits, but at the end of their weekend they agreed not to repeat the exercise and they kept their dirty business to the work of each book.

But that was then and over the intervening few years she had divorced from her husband.

She was childless in her mid-thirties and writing smut for an equally smutty man who put the books together and published them.

Lately the magic spark was slowly diminishing, slowly working its way out of the partnership and she knew it.

KRISTEN

The story had grown tiresome. She knew it, but kept typing anyway, she kept banging away on the keyboard as though if you hit the keys often enough they would produce some magic – they didn't.

It was something that had to get done. Missing deadlines didn't just mean that she would feel like shit in the morning, this was her job.

When Kristen had left her husband and moved into this loft apartment downtown, she knew that there were only two talents she had that she could use to get some quick money.

The first was selling her body, the second was writing. And writing got her in to less trouble and was a lot safer so she had taken that path with Erik.

On the nightstand beside her computer, her phone lit up the dark room with silent surprise. She didn't have to look, she knew who it was.

She didn't answer, letting her voice mail collect the call.

"I still haven't heard from you and we need to publish now. You are two weeks behind, Kristen", pleaded a familiar voice.

Of course, who the hell else would be calling her at this time of night? Erik was her writing partner and owner of a website selling erotica called 'Dirty Words'.

Before Kristen had started writing for him the website had been populated by his own erotic works - cheap, quick porn in words that sold in reasonable numbers each week.

But Erik complained he was burnt out and writing the same crap all the time. He admitted that he needed someone to help him, someone to fill in the froth of the ideas he came up with.
Kristen was the right girl in the right spot at the right time, she was lucky.

She communicated with him, after a few back and forths; she had suggested and ultimately sold him on the idea of her writing some of his content for him – becoming his erotic fiction ghost writer.

It had started with stories that Kristen could write for him quickly. Erik paid her fifty dollars a pop plus a commission of a few percent. He would tell her the characters, describe what they would do and then encourage her to go for it, being as dirty as she wanted.

She knew she could be making ten times that much selling her pussy, but this was keeping her away from people who might complicate her life, and more importantly from danger. And she was good at this.

After many years of marriage, preceded by a healthy sexual youth full of variety she had plenty of rich, dirty and disgusting material to keep her going – at least at first during the early years.
She enjoyed the writing; it distracted her from the pain of her life. It had allowed Kristen to pay her rent and buy a food.

Things quickly changed, though, as their new work combination took off and became quite popular. It wasn't on the best seller stands but she was soon making a thousand dollars a week from her efforts and this was a comfortable living.

Of course, comfortable had meant excesses in her life from time to time, and she took to drinking to ease her over her emotional problems, she was drinking beer heavily at first and then the harder stuff.

She would drink heavily, alone, and use the drunkenness as her excuse to be more creative. It worked, but it also meant sleeping in, feeling like shit when she awoke and being slow during the day. The side effect of her heavy drinking was that her output started slowing down and her imagination dimmed a bit.

Now she was struggling to finish every story and regularly falling behind their schedule. Erik often had to call her to get her back on track, he was being very tolerant of her but it was starting to piss him off.

On this particular day he had already called her many times as they had an urgent deadline to meet.

The fifth time Erik had called, it was twelve forty five. By then he was screaming that she was a stupid cunt and telling her she could forget about working for him ever again. She replied by emailing him the story.

A few minutes later, he called again.

"You're late," he said.

"I know," she said, trying to sound out of breath.

"My car broke down and I left my phone at home. I had to walk all the way up Ventura Ave just to find someone to--"

"Shut up! I told you when we started this that there would be no excuses."

"I-I-I know," she stammered. "I'm sorry."

"This shit you're sending me. It's garbage. I can barely sell it. It's nothing like what you used to write. What's wrong with you, where has your sexual spark gone?"

Kristen thought about some of her previous stories. They were better. Her favourite one featured a stripper at a party who decided to take things to the next level with five horny college students.

It had been her first time writing about double penetration. In all the years she had been married, she had always secretly hoped that her husband would come home drunk with one of his buddies and that they would take turns on her like the characters in her story. But of course he never did. Mormons, after all, were not known for their sexual adventures.

"What happened to you, Kristen? You remember that story about the utility worker?"

Yea, she remembered it all right. The story had been called Hot Wire. First the utility worker had watched, then he came in and what started as a rape ended as a bondage experience like none other - one that left both parties cumming hard. The memory of the story deepened Kristen's longing ache, her pussy began to warm and she could feel herself getting wet. She hadn't had a good fucking for years – not since their weekend fuck session and definitely not during her marriage. But at least it had been better than the dry spell since the divorce.

"Now that was a good story," he said. "That was probably one of my best sellers, you know!"

Something inside Kristen began to awaken. She started feeling the old urges. They had been strong before, back when she still wrote good stories, but even stronger before she got hitched.

On prom night she had sucked Graham Home's dick and then kissed Alahna 'Z something' with the cum still in her mouth. And that had just been during the limo ride. She had been different then, more exploratory, more adventurous and less hung up and serious.

"Did you like it, Erik? Did you like that story? Did it give you an erection?"

She took this path to take the heat off herself, but just for a split second she was aroused thinking of how she used to excite him sexually with her words. She wished she could get him into bed again and do all those dirty things they wrote about.

"What?"

"When you were reading that story were you thinking about me and grabbing your cock? Did you imagine me reaching into your pants and pulling out that beautiful cock of yours and playing with it? Is that an idea that still excites you Erik, it did back then you know. You used to get off all the time with the words I wrote for you.
Don't you think we have both lost something lately?"

Kristen even surprised herself as she said this. She must have surprised Erik even more because he didn't say a damn thing.

"You know when I wrote that I got so wet that I had to lay in the bathtub all night and rub my pussy until I couldn't cum anymore. I used to love those days, Erik, I used to love getting horny for you, writing messages to you and knowing you would take it out and whack off for me. You know it used to drive me to such excitement that I would be sore. What happened to us, why aren't we like that anymore?"

Silence again.

"Remember? Mostly I used my fingers, but sometimes I'd use something else and I would text you and tell you all about it, and sometimes I would take a photo and message it to you so you could see what I was up to. I used to love how I would drive you crazy with my pussy, and how you loved to see me pushing things into it for you. I loved it when you took control and just made me do outrageous sexual things!"

Silence.
And then, "What else did you use?"
A wicked smile appeared on Kristen's face. She was in control again and it felt good.

She hadn't been in control for so long that she had almost forgotten what it felt like.

"A big, black dildo. It was ten inches long and soooo thick and I could take it all for you. But it's just not the same, Erik. Nothing feels like a real cock sliding into your pussy, nothing feels as good as your hard dick sliding in and out of my soaking wet pussy," she purred as she aroused herself with the thoughts and words. She let her hand drop to her lap, she could feel the heat and dampness emanating from between her legs.

"Are you hard right now, Erik? Do you have a real cock to slide into my pussy, a gorgeous hard dick?"

She could hear Erik rustling with the phone. His breathing had deepened and all the authority in his voice was gone. She wondered if his cock was in his hand already, she hoped he was stroking it off as she spoke to him. She imagined the look of it, the smell, the heat.

"Yeah," he said. "I'm hard. What do you want me do with it?"

Oh yes, she was definitely in control.

"I'll tell you what. There's a hotel about thirty minutes from my place. And Erik, you'd better hurry. It's called the Narrows Hotel. I'll leave my name with the clerk so they'll be expecting you and don't let me down, I need a good fuck, right now!"

She quickly changed and applied some perfume in strategic places. She was amazed how fast this had all come together. She didn't want to be late, she needed to get her shit together for this and fuck like she had never fucked before – this was going to be a saving her career fuck!

She knew she needed this to get her mind back on the job, to engage in outrageous and forbidden sex so she could be back on the right path.

She raced downstairs and jumped into her old Volvo and sped off across town for her sexy rendezvous. She knew Erik was married, it was one of the reasons why they had never repeated their original rendezvous, but she didn't care, that was his wife's problem. She needed sex, with him and she was going to do it!

Half an hour later, Kristen entered the hotel room and took all the blankets from the bed. She walked around the room unscrewing all the light bulbs except for the one in the bathroom and she drew the blinds so the room was nice and dark.

She wondered whether she should get naked and jump into bed or was that being too slutty.

What would one of her heroines do in her books? Would one of those slutty girls get it all off and wait with their legs open – yeh, probably. They were usually all very easy lays, just as guys wanted, just as guys hoped.

FUCKING

Erik, to his credit, showed up 15 minutes later.

She smiled to herself, knowing he would have to have sped to get there so quickly. The front desk had given him a key as per her instructions and he slipped into the room, his hand going for the light switch.

It did nothing.

Fucking useless cheap hotel, he muttered to himself.

He was feeling excited but he also felt harassed and as though everything had shifted to Kristen's favour.

He had reminded himself all the way across town that she had been writing unimaginative crap lately and that she needed to get her act together and start producing real content.

He wanted her, he wanted to fuck her brains out, but he also needed her to write better content. He hadn't thought his ideas were that bad, he just reasoned that the problem was her writing had turned to crap. It was her fault.

Anyhow, his love life at home had been non-existent lately so he was happy to be having this sexual distraction.

He waited at the door for his eyes to adjust but even then was still apprehensive, where the fuck was she, or was this some kind of setup and she wasn't even there.

"Hello?" he asked hopefully.

"I'm here. Come in baby."
"I, umm, I want the light, where is it," asked Erik.

"No, it's better this way. I left the bathroom light alone, get in there and take a shower. I want you clean, before we get dirty, real dirty. When you are finished join me in the bed, I am naked and wet and dying to get into it, so hurry up. You'll find a mask by the sink. Put it on when you're done."

"A mask?"

"I want to pretend I've never seen you and you've never seen me. For tonight, we're just two characters in a story. Let's imagine we are in one of our stories."

"It doesn't matter who you are. All that matters is that you're mine."

Erik didn't need any more convincing. He went into the bathroom and undressed and then jumped into the shower. He didn't take long, he was eager and as he walked into the gloom of the bedroom towards the bed his cock was already

stirring and becoming hard.
He could see a little stream of moonlight shining in through
the window and running over a naked thigh that lay on the
bed. He remembered that thigh.

"Come. Lay down next to me," she said seductively.

Erik was nervous, but he once again did as he was told. His
arm reached out, seeking her, and upon feeling the smooth
silkiness of her skin, he lay down next to her. She wasted no
time in taking what she wanted. She wanted his dick, she
wanted it inside her body and she wanted to be satisfied.

Erik felt her warm body shift next to him, until she was on
top of him. Her hips straddled him and she could feel his
dick begin to harden. Kristen leaned down, until her bare
breasts were crushed in to his chest. She knew he would get
very hard as her tits rubbed on him. She reached down
between her legs and felt the cock she had used years before,
and she stroked it. She knew what it looked like; it was
average length, uncut and smooth – and very thick.

She kissed him, softly at first, her lips merely brushing his as
they familiarized themselves again.
She could taste the clean of freshly washed skin on his lips
and he tasted the cherry of her lip gloss.
The kisses started slow, but soon his arms were around her
and she parted her lips to let his tongue dance with hers. Her
mouth opened invitingly, she wanted him so much.
As she opened her mouth for him she could feel her pussy
swell and open as well, it wanted to be fed, badly. She made
a mental note to remember that feeling for the next book.
Erik continued to passionately attack her mouth, he seemed
desperate, and that pleased her.

His hands ran up and down her back, one holding her by the
neck, the other squeezing her ass, and Kristen responded by

grinding her pussy down against his growing cock. She gasped, the sound leaving her mouth and entering his. It was the type of thing that she wrote about and now it was happening for real. What she hadn't captured in her writing recently was the hunger, the desperation - instead she had just been writing the mechanical act, the sexual fact. Now she felt the raw animal lust inside her and it was burning between her legs.

She slid her body up and down, teasing his cock. Suddenly she was moving again and she rubbed her pussy over his belly, then over his chest and finally her knees rested on either side of his head.
He felt her warm, wet pussy press down onto his face. He could smell the alluring fragrance of her cunt on his face. His tongue reached for her slit eagerly. She allowed him to lick her clit then ground down onto him. His hands cupped her ass again as he fought to pull her even closer.
Her cunt flowed upon him with a wetness he couldn't keep up with. She was gushing all over him with her excitement. The excess from her vagina was coating his face, making it slick and sweet and so fragrant. He loved her scent, her sexual aroma.

She held his head in her fingers and pushed and rubbed hard against him. He could feel the tension in her body, he could feel the excitement. She started moaning. She was getting hot and sweaty and then it hit her – she came in a loud crescendo of excitements. It was the first time that night, but she would make sure it wouldn't be the last. In fact it was her first time with a man for quite a long time!

Her body rocked hard on top of him as she fucked herself on his face, only slowing down when her body no longer convulsed with pleasure.
She just sat on him, rubbing her clit slowly on his face as she wound down. The pleasure had been so intense, so beautiful.

Once her strength returned, she shifted her body so that she could reach his cock with her mouth while her pussy remained on his face. Eric was close to exploding when she grasped him with her hand.

She gave his cock a few quick strokes then took the head into her mouth, allowing her tongue to roll along its length.

She could sense Erik moaning with her oral attention, she could feel his groans into her cunt as his excitement increased. Her body tingled with every moan.
She loved it and it encouraged her to suck his dick harder.
She imagined him cuming in her mouth, the streams of sticky male cream being shot down her throat with the power of his orgasm.
She gushed all over his face as she imagined his orgasm, as she waited for it to erupt inside her.
She wanted to be used like this, she wanted to be a cum slut, she wanted the man to empty his balls into her mouth, and she was going to swallow it all.
She hoped he had a full load, she wanted to be such a slut, she needed to ignite and excite those feelings.

She couldn't believe how wild she had become. In her mind she was out of control, she knew anything would be possible in this fuck session.
She sucked like a wild whore; she wanted to blow him good, to give him a blow job that would sit in his memory for years. She was bobbing up and down so much that she was gagging.
She heard his breathing increase in tempo, she could feel his body starting to fuck her mouth more desperately, and then the moment she had wanted for so long - he forced her head down onto his prick as he released the streams of semen into her throat. She nearly choked he was filling her with so much sperm, but she didn't care, she loved being used like this.

He emptied into her mouth, using her orifice for his milk, and then she lowered her head to take him even deeper into her mouth, swallowing his cum.

Every drop passed right down her throat and she kept sucking until she felt him begin to grow limp. She was happy; she had succeeded in pleasing him, and being a dirty little slut in the process.

Lost in his own orgasm, Erik had almost forgotten about the pussy on his face. She reminded him by nearly crushing him with her hips.

She lapped at his cock, slowly sucking the tip, licking the semen that was slowly dribbling from the end of his uncut prick, while her hands cupped him.

A shudder ran through her body as his finger started to toy playfully with her asshole.

She had never liked her asshole being penetrated, but the feeling of it being played with was electric and she was in the mood to let herself go completely.

After all, if she was going to write about a woman, or man, wanting to take it up the ass, she needed to get into this sort of thing more.

She sucked on him again, giving his limp dick a proper blow job by bobbing her head up and down, her hand keeping him erect.

She was surprised that he responded so well to her oral actions, or maybe it was because she was letting him lick her asshole.

She did this until he was hard again, and then she slid once more along his body and now was ready for his dick inside her.

She held his cock and guided it expertly into her dripping vagina, she allowed the entirety of his cock to slide into her pussy. She gasped with delight at feeling so full and winced at how stretched and torn her unused pussy felt. It was like losing her virginity for a second time, but she loved it!

Erik didn't allow her time to adjust to his cock before grabbing her hips and thrusting in to her. He was eager to make her cum, so he held her hips and made her grind on him, rubbing her clit over his body as they fucked. It felt so good for her, so very, very good. It had been so long and she revelled in this renew experience.

"Yes," she cried. "Fuck me! Fuck me hard! I want it all, I need this, fuck me, baby!"

Erik was happy to oblige, pushing his cock as far as possible into her womanhood and thrusting hard to heighten her pleasure. Kristen moaned loudly as she was fucked and it wasn't long before she had her first vaginal orgasm for a long time.

When she was finished she collapsed on top of him, exhausted and totally spent. Her body was covered in sweat, she was puffing and panting, she was no longer a spring chicken.

SURPRISE

Erik, however, was not finished and had been very aroused watching her take her fun from his cock. He wanted some forbidden pleasure.

He rolled her over onto her knees and licked her asshole, making it nice and wet and ready.

Kristen gasped, "Oh no, Erik, your cock will be too big. You will hurt me, don't do it."

"I want your ass Kristen, take it bitch, open up your dirty ass for me and let me use it. I want to fill it with cum, I want you walking out of her tonight with my cum leaking out of every hole, you slut!"

Kristen was stunned by his language, but knew she had to submit, she had brought him here, after all, to get their sex writing invigorated.

She obediently let Erik lick her asshole and then felt him start to mount her. She felt him sliding his thumb in and out to open her up, and then she could feel the thick, blunt end of his prick trying to force its way up her ass.

She screamed as he pulled her hair and thrust hard and deep up her bum, but she let him have his way. He obviously wanted this, she was going to be submissive and let him use her completely.

His cock felt enormous as he pounded away on her butt. She hoped he would cum inside her soon, she didn't know how much of this anal punishment she could take.

Maybe that's what it was, she wondered. Was this Erik's way of punishing her for her wayward writing lately?

She screamed more loudly as he hammered her ass, she was sure she would be broken by his cock. Then she felt him tense and he bellowed as he came like a wild animal, pumping his seed into her tight little fuck hole.

When he was finally done, she collapsed forward and lay there, totally abused.

Minutes later, surprisingly, there was a knock on the door and two men entered. It was the guy from the front counter and some other man.

"Hey lady, if you are going to make this much noise, you have to share – house rules, baby."

Kristen was horrified and clutched at the sheets and looked at Erik.

He just laughed, pulled his cock out of her slimy asshole and said to the men, "Ok, guys it's your turn to use her now. Fuck her hard, it's what she needs and it's what I am paying you for. She needs new ideas for writing erotica so use her until you are both done."

"What the fuck," started Kristen as she saw Erik dressing.

He turned to her and replied, "You said you wanted to get into more kinky stuff so you could write more imaginatively. So when I came in tonight I told the counter guy to come up here after half an hour and fuck your brains out. These two are going to give you a threesome."

"Enjoy it, baby, I am going home. And I sure as hell look forward to your next story in a few days."

Erik left for home and his loving wife, leaving Kristen to live out her slut fantasies as the two men used her every hole for the next three hours. At the end of it she was a cum dribbling mess, but over the next few months her writing didn't lack any passion, or imagination.

4 HEAVEN

The world sucked for Alan, he was an overweight, middle aged man and there wasn't a great deal of excitement left for him in his life. It was just boring drudgery every day. One day as he stepped out the elevator, the world turned a blinding white and suddenly he was somewhere else, with naked women and outrageous sexual habits. After an evening of torrid love making he had a decision to make...

ALAN

Alan walked to his dreary government job, as he did each day, trying to get up the spirit to be happy, the spirit to go on, and the spirit to be positive.

It was a struggle.

The world sucked for Alan, he was an overweight, middle aged man and there wasn't a great deal of excitement left for him in his life. It was just boring drudgery every day.

He turned the corner, bid the footman a good morning and entered the cavernous foyer of the enormous government building. It was new, modern and totally without character. He expected it looked like something straight out of 1984.

Once inside the building, Alan greeted the security guard, Alfred, as he did every morning and they exchanged the usual comments of amazement about the weather even though the weather was completely predictable these days.

Alfred looked at Alan and asked, "Excuse my rudeness, Sir,

but are you feeling alright; you look a little pale this morning? Not feeling well, perhaps?"

"Ah, no, Alfred, I am fine thank you."

Alan strode across the marbled floor to the bank of elevators and pressed the 'up' button.

The elevator doors opened in front of him and he entered. As the doors were closing he saw his boss walking quickly towards him.

Oh shit, thought Alan, he will want that bloody report.

He feigned to press the 'open doors' button, but instead hit the 'shut doors' and the two steel doors closed and excluded all other occupants.

It was a reasonable mistake, especially when these days the only options were two smart arse symbols that one first had to decipher before pressing.

The elevator moved smoothly on its journey to the 16th floor, Alan felt momentarily relieved to have escaped from his boss, although he noticed he was sweating.

Then just as the elevator arrived at its destination Alan felt suddenly very dizzy, everything around him started to rotate and then spin.

The spinning motion changed its plane of alignment and started tilting, he lost his balance completely, falling to his knees to try to recover his composure.

There was a swift jolt in his chest and then a blinding light in front of him and the elevator door opened, a glaring white light replacing the expected office setting.

Alan couldn't stand; he crawled slowly out of the elevator and into this white light environment.

Once out of the lift he felt better, the spinning stopped, his balance returned and he was able to stand.

The light was so bright; he held his hand over his eyes in an attempt to see around him.

Gradually the surroundings cleared, but where there should have been a modern 21st century office there was instead some kind of platform and he was standing on it.

Alan looked about him, the sky was amazingly clear and blue, there was a scent of tropical paradise in the air and all about him he could see incredibly beautiful women.

This was obviously not his work floor, had he perhaps pressed the wrong button and alighted at the executive floor?

WHERE AM I?

He seemed to be standing on some beach sand, it was warm and soft.

There appeared to be music coming from a hut nearby and

people were dancing, many of them naked.

To his left there was a small tropical hut bar, he walked over and sat down and looked for a waiter, he needed a drink for sure.

Then he noticed on the bartop a single glass, it said 'click me' to have a cocktail.

Click me? he thought, what is that shit?

He reached out to touch it and somehow a menu came up in thin air in front of his eyes and it invited him to select from many options, including one that said 'Drink'.

By thinking that he wanted to select that option, somehow it was selected and before he knew it, a copy of the drink was in his hand and full of coloured liquid.

He brought the glass to his lips and sipped the drink.

It was sensational; it was heavenly - and nice and intoxicating too.

He took a long drink and then set the glass on the counter. As he released it from his hand he noticed the glass rim had lipstick on it.

Fuck, that's a bit slack really isn't it, he thought to himself. At least the bar staff could have cleaned the damn glass – slack bastards.

Again he looked around for bar staff, but there were none.

As he turned to his glass again he caught sight of his image in a small mirror on the bar, and he froze.

He looked around him, looked back at the image and then looked down at himself, and nearly died.

For all of his life Alan had been a portly gentleman, but now when he looked down he was a woman, and an attractive woman at that.

Whereas moments ago he had been 53 years old, and a male, now he was in his mid-twenties, an attractive 25 year old woman.

He was stunned, had he fallen down and hit his head and was now in some absurd and perverse dream?

This was not possible.

He stood up, he looked at himself again.

He was tall, slim with attractively sized breasts; he was wearing a see through mesh vest and tight black leggings with white leather ankle boots.

His hair was short, shaped forward on the sides and black and he looked fucking fantastic - except Alan knew he was really a man and he was looking in the mirror and seeing a woman!

He looked around to make sure nobody was looking directly at him and tried to recover his composure.

He needed another drink; this was all too much for him.

He motioned towards the glass again and selected 'Drink'

and his glass filled up.

He liked that idea. He didn't know where he was but he wished he could take that nifty little invention back home with him – he would make a mint!

He took the glass and stood up. To his left there was a small bridge heading out to the sky and a sign that read, 'Lovers Leap'.

Curious, Alan walked onto the bridge and out along it. As he made his way along the ten feet of its length he realized that he was on some kind of sky platform and it was fucking thousands of yards down.

He couldn't even see the bottom!

Not a great fan of heights he eased himself back onto the terra firma of the main platform.

Nothing made sense to him in this odd world. He continued taking in the scene, the smells and the sounds.

He listened to the announcer key in the next song, J'ai Envie De Toi.

It seemed to be some French radio station, was he in France? Maybe that explained it all, somehow the damned frogs had kidnapped him. If he was in France, things had changed since he had last visited. It now seemed like heaven - they had clearly moved ahead of his nation.

The place had atmosphere, energy, there was thumping, pumping euro trance music blaring through the air.

Alan moved back to the safety of the bar, this world was too unusual for him to walk around, who knew what trouble he might get into.

He watched the women walking around the club and saw one appear out of thin air onto some mat about ten feet in front of him. It seemed to be some focal point, some kind of entry point, perhaps?

How the fuck did they do that, he wondered.

Another woman nearby just turned into vapour and disappeared.

This was clearly some bizarre dream, he reasoned, people don't just appear and disappear in normal life.

He took another drink and was trying to observe as much of this odd place as possible. He then noticed a sign near the entry mat. It read 'Shemale and Lesbian Love Club'.

What the fuck, that explained it. He was in some fucking weirdo club. There would have to be a manager somewhere, a door to the outside. He looked around for assistance, but there was none.

It was then that he noticed a woman standing a few feet away and looking at him.

SUZI

She was stunning. She was petite, and brunette with lips that men would kill for and a body to match it all.

He noticed that he still seemed attracted to women even though he was technically a woman, somehow - so that was good.

She smiled at him.

She offered her hand and said, "I'm sorry I wasn't here to meet you, I was held up with another person and couldn't get back here on time. I hope you aren't feeling too disoriented and uncomfortable. But, to the best of our knowledge this is exactly what you wanted so here you are, it should be familiar to you."

The woman continued, "And I am sorry for being so rude and not introducing myself to you, Alahna."

"My name is Suzi."

Alahna? Who the fuck was Alahna, he wondered and then it occurred to him that maybe Alan the man had become Alahna the woman - what a world!

The woman gave him that melting smile again, she nodded, "Yes honey, your name is Alahna. Didn't you get an information pack when you arrived today? Oh my, we have slipped up, haven't we? I am so sorry."

"Here come with me, it's nearly time for the sunset, you will love it."

She reached for Alan's hand and walked with him past many people dancing, couples kissing and past the elevated huts on the beach sand. They walked through an area of palm

48

trees and came to the edge of the platform but on the other side.

"Well honey, four times a day the sun rises and falls here, it's time for the sunset."

She held his hand and stood close to him. Alan watched as the bright red globe descended through some broken clouds near the horizon and then shot its rays across the ocean and across this weird world as it sunk into the waters many miles away.

Alan was amazed at this place, sunset four times a day? Where the fuck was he, it clearly wasn't on Earth. And how had he gone from an elevator at work to this crazy land?

Suzi took the lead again, "Here, lets' find somewhere with a little more privacy."

She led him through the palms and then they came out into a serene setting. In front of them there was a little hut surrounded by water with a wooden bridge going across to it. As the darkness of night descended, torches flared up and their flames flickered to light the way.

It was an extraordinary scene. On the island there was a bed, lit by the flares of the torches and the moonlight. What a fantasy world it was for Alan.

Suzi turned to him and asked, "So, how are you this fine evening, if you don't mind us starting again on the right footing?"

"Oh great, and you? I am still trying to figure out where I am and how I got her, by the way."

"I'm doing very well, Alahna. Don't worry about why you are here or how you got here, you are in paradise now. Its heaven here and there is nothing to worry about ever again."

Alan took her at her word and relaxed a little, she didn't seem that threatening.

Suzi continued, "Hey today, I'm out exploring, looking around. I am possibly looking for some fun, you know." And she then winked at him.

She smiled and added, "You have some interesting fantasies, you know, Alahna."

"Fantasies?" replied Alan incredulously and wondered what the fuck this silly woman was up to now.

"Yes my sweet, all your deepest and most secret fantasies are out there for all to read about, it's in your profile."

Profile he thought, what the fuck was his profile?

Suzi showed him. "You just look here, honey, on any person and you can see information about them."

She pointed to her head and said, "Go on, look at my profile."

Alan did as she directed and it was true, another pop up menu revealed itself over her head and he could read all about her.

"And if you think about your own profile you will see it is there and you can read it, but you can't edit it."

"It tells us all about you, and reveals everything about your life, and what you want and fantasize about. Nothing can be hidden.'"

"OMG," said Alan, "How did they get there, it is all so revealing, and my darkest dirtiest secrets!"

"Oh, that's ok, it's just part of the deal when you arrive, honey, just part of the package. Everyone who arrives here has the same thing."

"Oh, and speaking of packages..." Suzi giggled and looked down at his groin.

Alan looked down and saw he had a bulge in his panties.

OMG, he had a fucking cock as well as being a woman, what sort of creature was he?

And then he realized - he must be a shemale as this was a shemale and lesbian club.

Suzi smiled and gave him a cheeky wink.

"I must say, I do find your dirty little fantasies quite attractive, honey."

Alan blushed, fuck those fantasies could get me into SO much trouble, he thought.

"Don't worry about it sweetie, it's better to be a bit extreme than mundane."

"What," he shrieked, "Extreme, where?"

Suzi threw her head back and laughed wickedly.

"Oh well, it's putting it out there."

"Well it's like this, Alahna. And here, this is my fantasy, look!"

The next moment a large photo of a naked Suzi appeared in front of Alan, he didn't know how. It just hovered there in thin air. Not only was she gloriously naked, and he loved the view, but she was also wearing a slim penis attached to her body.

Alan sighed, "Hmmmm, what a gorgeous fantasy, Suzi. You are quite a delicious little thing, aren't you?"

Suzi giggled and innocently smiled.

"Well, it's nice to dream you know and have these little fantasies to keep one going."

"That's true," agreed Alan thoughtfully.

Suzi suddenly turned provocatively to Alan and removed her top.

She was straight in front of him and her amazing tits just hung there in front of his hungry eyes. He couldn't keep his eyes off her stunning boobs as they performed their gravity defying act.

They were the most perfect tits he had ever seen, truly perfect in every possible way.

"Hmmm, now that's a lovely view," he said trying to be casual about it.

He looked at her, his mind considering what he would love

to do with this woman.

"Oh, you are a naughty boy, I was thinking the same thing! You must be psychic."

"How did you read my mind like that?" responded Alan.

"Don't you worry about that darling, you know I can be a little naughty too, I am not always miss goodie two shoes angel."

As Alan stared at the angelic, bare breasted woman, he felt the familiar swelling below starting to take over.

"You will get me all excited standing there like that, Suzi. You have such a lovely body.

Suzi responded, 'Well, that is the whole point honey. It's what you want."

Suzi stepped forward and kissed Alan softly on his lips; electricity ran through his body like never before in his life and his cock was stirring below.

She ran her finger tips along the curve of his body, his skin tingling, his body longing for her.

All Alan could do was moan louder with each touch, with each caress.

"You will make me too excited soon and you will see more of me and my fantasy might pop up." He laughed nervously as he was already hard.

Suzi swallowed, "That would be horrible, I don't think!"

"Come, let's go lay down on this bed and relax together and get to know each other better and live out some of those fantasies. The night is young."

"Perhaps we should sit on the bed and chat a bit, or something?"

"Hmmmm, oh yes, please," came Alan's swift reply to Suzi's offer.

SEX!

The two girls walked over to the spacious bed in the middle of the tropical hut, and then lay down next to each other, Suzi running her fingers along Alahna's body.

"Oh, that is nice, Suzi, your fingers on my tingling skin, so sexy."

Suzi settled in and rested her head on Alahna's warm breast. She moaned softly into the skin.

She ran her tongue around the other woman's nipple, tasting it, teasing it with her lips, pulling it into erectness.

Alan, now Alahna, moaned and whispered, "Don't stop, honey, please don't stop." He was weak now, he had no resistance.

"Oh this is so amazing, Suzi, so perfect."

Suzi lifted her head and smiled. "I have a confession to

make, I have a bit of a kink, you know."

"Really?" replied Alahna, "You must tell me about it."

"Well," continued Suzi, "I enjoy helping people like you cum."

Alahna moaned, although he wondered what someone like him was?

"I also love the idea of making someone else cum, so maybe we could help each other?"

Suzi played her fingers run along Alahna's tummy, "You are so sexy."

"Carefully, Suzi, if you go any further down there you might have to watch out for a surprise."

Suzi purred into his ear, "I hope so."

She kissed Alahna softly on the cheek, and the lips, and then the mouth. Suzi kissed Alahna's tongue, slipping hers around her lover's lips.

Alahna moaned softly into her mouth as they kissed.

Suzi was eager, "I don't care if there is a cock or pussy between your legs as long as you have passion, my love."

Alahna kissed her red lipsticked mouth to show his passion. She brought her fingers to his mouth, Alahna sucked them longingly, one by one, their eyes looking deep into each other's.

"Hmmm, your fingers are so delicious, Suzi."

Suzi responded by rolling his now erect nipple in her fingers, teasing it, twisting it gently as she played with him. Alahna's nipples stood proudly erect, busting for her lips on them.

"Kiss them, Suzi." His lover responded by applying her mouth to each nipple in turn, sucking it gently, fondly, tasting it."

Suzi's lips pinched them, sucked them softly and tugged on them. Alahna held her head gently against his body.

Suzi then moved back up to Alahna's mouth and kissed him passionately and desperately.

As she kissed the new shemale, she let her fingers go into Alahna's panties and she pulled out his cock, it was already hard and waiting to please.

She wrapped her fist around his cock and started to stroke him, slowly. She looked into his eyes to see if there was a reaction. Alahna had closed his eyes and was groaning with every stroke on his very hard cock, his shemale cock.

"Oh fuck, Suzi that feels like nothing on Earth."

She giggled, "that's right, honey, like nothing on Earth."

As Suzi stroked his cock, she knelt over him so she could look down as she performed her task. She liked pleasing her new client.

"Your dick is so magnificently hard, Alahna, so hot in my hand and so exciting. It feels beautiful." She leant forward and took a suck of his cock, and ran her tongue over the tip, sucking on the eye of his penis. Alahna moaned loudly.

"Hmmm, you like that do you, sweetie? Maybe you would like to come in my mouth as well, I would love to blow you and swallow all of your hot sperm."

Alahna nodded pathetically, having lost all control.

Suzi smiled and lowered her head back down onto the hot salty penis and began to bob up and down on the scorching flesh, eager to bring Alahna to climax.

"Oh god, yes, that feels so good, please don't stop, I want to come in your mouth, suck me off, please."

Alahna pushed Suzi's head down further onto his cock and started to thrust upwards in animal desperation. He needed this, he needed this pleasure, and he needed to empty his balls into her warm mouth.

"Oh god, darling, that is so good, I am getting close now."

Suzi sucked harder and bobbed up and down so fast she was starting to gag. She wanted to blow this shemale, she wanted Alahna's load in her mouth. She wanted so desperately to take all his come.

"Oh god, don't stop, I am nearly there, coming soon," cried out Alahna as he pumped her face.

"Oh fuck yes, oh fuck, fuck, fuck," he cried.

Suzi moaned on his cock and gulped it down even further; it was now at the back of her throat.

Then Suzi moved a finger up between Alahna's thighs and ran it around the entrance to his anus. When she heard

Alahna moan louder, she inserted it slowly, without lubrication, pushing it deeper into his ass until her finger was thrusting wildly up into his bottom.

"Oh fuck yes, so good, I am coming, I am coming, yes, yes, yes, yes!"

Alahna held Suzi's head hard down over his dick and in one swift action pumped his cock deep and unleashed his torrent of hot sperm down her throat. He pumped constantly, the fluid streaming into her, choking her, suffocating her.

Alahna's semen was leaking from Suzi's lips as she struggled to keep up with the flow of sticky white cream being pumped into her body.

Finally, Alahna was done and his cock started to grow limp. Suzi let it fall out of her mouth and then holding it tenderly in her fingers, she proceeded to lick it clean, sucking the dripping sperm from the tip, squeezing gently to eke out every last drop of white love cream. She kissed it lovingly on the tip and then moved over to Alahna and kissed him on the lips.

"Hmmm, I am glad we did that," she said to her lover.

"But now it's my turn for a little pleasure.

She rolled Alahna over and moved him into position so he was on his knees and his ass was up in the air.

Suzi tenderly applied her tongue to his anal sphincter, licking around the forbidden hole, tasting him, taking in his rich scent. She removed her tied skirt and let it fall and then in moments a large and swollen penis slowly appeared, where before there had been a neatly trimmed vagina. As she knelt with an erect penis behind Alahna she continued to slurp away enthusiastically on his anal passage, pushing her tongue into it, twisting her tongue, fucking his ass with her tongue. She loved attending to him, and she was looking forward to using him. As she licked, Alahna groaned into the pillow.

"Oh fuck me, baby, use me," he cried out to Suzi as he grew desperate to be used. He was overcome with a need to be submissive, anally submissive for his lover.

"Oh yes, my love, I have every intention of fucking you hard and using your ass. Be patient, I am just preparing you for my cock."

Suzi then moved in behind Alahna and rubbed her rigid penis across the cheeks of his ass. Alahna moaned, sensing what was going to happen next.

He had always wondered what this would be like, had fantasized about it, and now his angel was about to slide her cock deep into his ass.

Alahna tensed for the moment, but Suzi told him to relax, to let it happen. She soothed his ass with her hands, and then guided her cock to the forbidden entrance, Alahna's little dark hole.

She pressed slowly, forcing her bulbous penis head into his tight sphincter. Just the tip of her dick was in, no more. She continued to push slowly, and gently, and urged Alahna to relax to make it easier.

Finally she felt Alahna open up inside and her cock eased up into the fruity passage.

"Oh my god, that feels so good," called out Alahna as he felt the first few strokes in his ass.

"Oh yes, I love it, I have always wanted this."

"I know sweetie, we know all about your little fantasies, that's why I am here. Now relax and let me take you completely, I want to push my cock deep into you, I want to feel the walls gripping my length."

Alahna groaned louder, his moans muffled by the pillow as his ass was being pumped, but still clearly audible.

Suzi was now working up a rhythm, her cock sliding in and out of the slimy rear passage of the shemale in front of her.

"Do you like taking it in the ass, Alahna, do you like a cock up your bum?" she called out as she rammed her length into him.

"Oh fuck yes," he replied, "don't stop, I need this so much, I need a good fucking. Fuck me hard, fuck me harder!"

"Take my ass, use it baby, screw it."

Suzi reached forward and pulled Alahna's hair with her fingers, making Alahna squeal as she was pumped hard.

"Take my dick, bitch, take it up the ass."

"Feel my balls bouncing against your ass as I pump you, fucking you, screwing your slutty asshole."

Alahna knew he was in heaven; the pleasure was

overpowering and mind blowing. He wanted to please Suzi, he wanted to give Suzi his ass and let her cum inside it. He wanted her sperm in his ass, he definitely knew that.

Suzi continued to plunge her cock into the available asshole, pumping hard as sweat starting to roll of her body in the heat of the tropical evening.

"Oh yes, baby, your ass is so tight, I am going to come soon, milk my balls for me with your ass, squeeze hard and make me blow inside you."

Alahna did as he was told, obediently, submissively - he wanted his lover to come inside his ass.

"Fuck me hard, Suzi, come inside me, please," he begged in complete desperation. He gave himself totally, her cock ravaging his virgin asshole for the first time, forcing it open, stretching it, hurting it and yet he loved every moment. This was heaven for Alahna, it was his sexual fantasy come true.

"Oh yes, I am coming, Alahna," called out Suzi desperately.

"Yes, do it, fill me, fill me up," came the eager reply.

Suzi held Alahna's hips and punched away at his ass with her cock, sliding it in and out, deeper and deeper and then she clutched him hard as he released into his body, wave after wave of hot seed.

When Suzi was done, and her cock fell out of Alahna's bottom, she lay down next to him and ran her fingers through his soft, feminine hair.

"I hope you enjoyed that sweetie, it was your fantasy."

"Oh god, yes," he replied, "that was the best sex ever in my life."

Suzi smiled, "well know that you also have female parts you will be able to experience many sensations in this place, my love."

"That's why we are all here, to help you live out your dreams, your needs and your sexual wants."

She kissed him tenderly and then said, " why don't you sleep my baby," and closed his eyes with her fingers.

DECISION

The next thing Alahna knew there was a bright light around him again, things were swimming around him, and there were noises, familiar noises, and familiar voices.

Slowly he opened his eyes; there was a doctor, a blurry doctor, discussing things with a blurry image of his wife.

He could just hear what they were saying.

The doctor seemed to be telling her that the worst was over, but they would have to monitor him for some time. The doctor also pointed out that some drip was critically important to his recovery and that the flow must not be stopped, even for a minute or he would die.

The two of them walked out the door and it closed.

Alan lay there and looked around. He could see some drip next to his bed; a liquid was going into his body.

The pondered the doctor's comments, and his future, and he pondered the experience he had just enjoyed.

Minutes later he managed to manoeuvre his fingers onto the tube that was going into his body. He pulled it out slowly and let it fall to the ground.

He hoped that there would be no alarm, or that he had enough time for his plan to work.

Moments later he opened his eyes to a blinding light. He hoped desperately that his plan had worked and he was now in a better place, the only place for him.

As his eyes focused he saw a smiling face, a familiar face. She leant forward and kissed him softly.

"I was hoping you would make the right choice, darling."

"Welcome back to Heaven."

5 THE GIRL WHO FARTED DURING SEX

I don't know what to say about this story. The title says it all in this short, true little tale. If you are brave, and in need of a good laugh, read on...

Hello.

Yes, I know you are probably laughing your heads off about the title of this ebook. How marvellous for you. You know, this was no laughing matter for me. It was quite serious for me at the time. But let's not spoil all the fun; let's do this in chronological order.

Once upon a time, I had a girlfriend, her name was Cheryl.

She was quite attractive, intelligent, hardworking and independent, quite a good catch actually. We had been going out together for about a month and things were going along nicely. We were seeing each other probably four or five nights a week, enjoyed each other's company and had great sex together.

It was a very encouraging relationship.

I really liked being with her, and she indicated she had similar feelings about our young love. I think we were approaching that stage where we would consider moving in together. We were past the "I love you stage", we had past that emotional hurdle, we were seeing each other so often it would save us time to live together.

She lived uptown, I lived downtown, and the commute was

a bitch. We alternated to make it fair. Sometimes we would end up in her apartment and I would stay over, other times she would stay the night at my place. It was cute.

One cold night in mid-winter we decided to stay at home and eat in as it was too cold outdoors. It was good snuggling weather. I decided to make a special night of it by cooking at my place. She brought the wine, I cooked.

She swept in the door, bringing the cold world with her as it clung to her coat. I helped her out of it, kissed her and we sat down to chat for a while.

Then she went to freshen up, I went back to the delectable chicken dish I was cooking and poured some wine for us. She returned, kissed me some more and we settled in for a night of love and contentment.

I was soon ready to serve dinner, a lovely chicken satay with fried rice and Chinese vegetables. It tasted quite nice even if I do say so myself. She loved it!

Her plate was soon demolished, and she wanted more. As I had cooked enough for a few meals there was plenty extra. I watched as she devoured the second helping I had made her.

She was content. We sat down and relaxed for a while, finishing the rest of the bottle of wine; I think she was getting nicely tiddly by the end.

Then we started to kiss, and kiss some more and we began to undress each other. As I removed her blouse I released her beautiful soft and warm breasts. They were a bit smaller than average, firm and well balanced. Her nipples were that lovely torpedo shape I loved to see in online porn pics. Even though we were in our early thirties, her belly was firm, her pubic mound trimmed neatly and her skin held the delicate fragrance of her perfume.

I am a man; of course I don't know what it was!

I removed the last of her clothing, as she commenced undressing me. As she slid down my underpants my hardened cock sprang to life, she stroked it lovingly for a few moments before bending forward to take it into her mouth. My cock melted as it entered her velvety mouth. She was very pleasing orally. I looked down and enjoyed the view, watching my enlarged penis slide in and out of her lipstick covered mouth. I closed my eyes to enjoy the sensation. I am sure I was moaning, it was delightful. I could have stayed there all night enjoying her attentions but that would be unfair and not very gentlemanly of me.

I stood up and moved over to the large soft rug in the middle of the room. I then lay down and drew her down with me so that she could continue her expert work on my dick. I positioned her so that I could get to her cunt, and started to lick it and kiss it.

It was wonderful. As she sucked my manhood, I enjoyed the full view of her vagina, I could smell its sweetness, bask in the view of her entrance, and enjoy eating her love folds.

It was heaven. As I licked and sucked and fingered her, she grew more and more excited.

She was gushing from time to time, she was so intense, and it aroused me greatly to see her so excited. My face was buried in her cunt, lapping up her love juices. I also licked her cute asshole with my tongue, gliding my tongue around its entrance, enjoying the kinky taste and aromas. I held her anus open with my fingers as she continued to work my cock, I was so aroused by the sight of her tiny puckered little bum hole.

And then it happened.

THE FART

I was staring straight at the hole when suddenly it opened, it flexed and a violent explosion of hot, noisy gas came charging out and smacked into my face.

My face had been inches from her ass. I felt the full force of her anal blast! It was hot, a hot wind blasted against my face. I can still today remember, intimately, exactly how it felt. I was shocked. I was stunned. And I was in a real pickle.

If I laughed, or ran away I could ruin her sex life forever.

I had to do the right thing. For the sake of the rest of mankind, I had to do the right thing.

I did what any man, hell bent on fucking, would do - I pretended it didn't happen.

Well, I tried to be polite and pretend it didn't happen. That worked for a few seconds.

Then came the stench. Oh my fucking god, it was the most

foul, the most disgusting fart I have ever smelt in my life and it had been blasted at me, full force, from inches away.

I had seen the fart. I had seen her ass open to do it. I had felt the hot gasses rush over my face. She had basically farted on my face!!!

And now I was smelling the most putrid, the most disgusting, foul stench you could ever imagine. How long could I survive and continue to pretend?

How long before I died. I was on the verge of death already. I had been trying not to breathe for a few minutes.

Agggggghhhhhhhh, I was sure I would have to die.

And then she must have got a whiff of the smell as well. She reacted instantly. She whirled around and hugged me urgently, saying how sorry she was and what a disgusting thing it was to do. She kept apologizing for minutes.

She especially apologized for the disgusting odour. What could I do? Clearly she hadn't intended to do the world's most putrid fart on my face. Clearly she hadn't even intended to fart at all. As she said, it just slipped out. She said she felt too happy and relaxed at the time, so it just happened.

Wow, good thing it was only the gas that came out and not the objects!

I hugged her; there was little else I could do. What could I do? It was an accident. But what an accident, and what a stench. Fuck me dead it was horrid?

You won't be surprise that the fart episode killed sex for the night.

We hugged, she apologized, and then finally she decided she should go home. I didn't argue.

What a moment in my life, having a woman fart on my head during sex. How would I ever forget that, how would she ever live it down? Would we survive? All very important questions, I assure you.

Well, to cut a long story short, we did survive, for a while. Mind you, for a few days she found excuses not to come around but finally love conquered the problem and we got on with our life together. I gotta say though, I don't think we engaged in oral for a while, at least not the oral involving my head between her legs kind of oral.

Over time we settled back into our routine, and sex came back into our lives.

Then one night we grabbed a take away at some chicken joint and went home. After some kissing and cuddling and wine, we went to bed and made hot passionate love. She sat on top of me and enjoyed an intense orgasm, and then she rolled over and lay on her side. I entered from behind and began to fuck her pussy.

My hands were on her lovely tits, my cock sliding in and out of her tight, wet cunt, it was fantastic.

I slammed into her hard, and then there was a popping noise that didn't quite enter my horizon.

I pounded her again, there was another popping noise. This

lodged into my brain but whilst the grey cells were trying to calculate the source of the noises, there were more with each thrust into her body.

I thrust, she popped.

I thrust again, she popped again.

I was so close I had to keep fucking, but my brain was recording the pops.

And then the stench hit me. Oh my fucking god. It had obviously taken a few moments to waft its way up to my nostrils. Now it was trying to kill me again. Once again I tried to continue like a true gentleman, but fuck the stench was killing me.

Then she smelt it.

She screamed.

She cried. She broke down in massive embarrassment.

She was mortified and so embarrassed.

And, of course, I missed out on my climax again.

I hugged her and assured her it was ok. Was it?? She was so upset and didn't know what to do. I told her not to run away but to stay.

She did. Oh god it was bad though. The smell was as bad as the first time when she had dropped her gas bomb right on my face. This girl had a problem, a big problem.

It took sometime before she recovered, a little. I tried to cheer her up by suggesting it was the chicken and wine combination. I think she liked that idea. At least she felt more in control if she knew what was causing it.

But what was I going to do?

Could I live my life with someone who could fart in my face anytime during sex?

Oh my....... that would be hard.

It started to put a barrier between us, even though she insisted it was the first time in her life that she had this problem.

We struggled along but I think the relationship was now doomed. Then one day she told me her mother was ill and she would have to go back west to look after her for a while. I don't know if that was the truth, or whether it was just her way of leaving me gracefully.

We kept in touch for a while, by mail and phone back in those days. Then she stopped calling.

Then she stopped writing.

And it was over.

I never heard from her again.

I don't know what happened to her problem, I don't know if she has it fixed or if she still farts away during sex. Poor husband if she does.

But I will never forget the sight of her ass opening and the hot gas blowing at my face. And I will never forget the stench, oh my fucking god it was horrid.

I hope she had a good life, good luck to her.

6 THE MAID

Brian had often fantasised about their having a maid, but was stunned when his wife actually arranged for one to move in with them. Of course, the inevitable happened, he fell in love with her but he did not expect the wild twisting of events that would follow, and he had not anticipated his wife's deception.

BRIAN

They were sitting in the sun one afternoon, yes it is possible to have a sunny afternoon in England, and he made one of his typical silly jokes.

He was feeling in the mood for a beer, but neither he nor his wife wanted to move.

"I suppose we need a maid," he joked.

His wife, who had heard him jokingly comment on this before, replied quickly, "Yes, a maid would be useful and she could also pull you off."

"Hmmm, what a lovely idea," Brian responded.

"Oh well, if you can afford a maid, go and get one and she can pull you off and suck you off, and pour your beer, I don't care anymore, I just want someone to clean the house."

Oh my, what a temptation, thought Brian.

Could he really afford to get a maid and could he get away with having sex with her?

Later that evening, just to provoke the issue since he was feeling cheeky and excited by the idea, he said to his wife, "And what sort of maid should we get, my darling?"

"I suppose she would have to be French, named Fifi, and wear a very short skirt and have a feather duster."

Brian was in such good form.

"I suppose she should also bend over often, maybe when I drop my hankie."

He laughed.

His wife said, "Or maybe she could be fifty years old, she could be a German woman called Helga and be built like a brick shithouse and when she pulls you off she does it to the sound of German marching music and your dick would be sore for a month."

She laughed; she always thought she was funny. He, of course, didn't see the humour in it.

He went back to his image of Fifi, sadly Helga kept interrupting.

Oh well, he sighed inwardly.

A few weeks later his wife came to him and said that she had seen an advert on the Internet for a maid. The woman was about forty, she wanted a live in position and didn't want much money since the live in would be worth a lot to her.

She was Irish and she wanted to spend twelve months with a household.

They looked over her details and Brian checked out her photos.

Actually she looked ok for a forty year old. It said she didn't have any kids and it showed. Her tits still looked firm and upright, they looked small and she was slim.

I wouldn't have minded giving her one, Brian thought.

But he didn't seriously think they would ever have a maid.

KATRINA

He was very surprised to find a few weeks later that they did indeed have a maid and her name was Katrina, she was the Irish girl.

His wife had organized everything; she said all he had to do was pay for it all.

He was introduced to Katrina and she was more attractive than in the advert.

She had lovely reddish, brown hair; it was mid length and curled into hug her face. He loved her accent. She was about five foot eight, small breasted and slim - for a middle aged woman, that is.

She seemed to be a happy woman.

She thanked them for giving her a chance; she said it was too hard finding decent employment in Ireland at the moment.

His wife showed her to her room; it was upstairs at the end of the house, in the spare room next to his study.

Brian carried her bags, under his wife's direction, to Katrina's room and they let her settle in.

Once they were back downstairs his wife asked, "What do you think?"

Brian shrugged and said, "I suppose time will tell, we will have to see how she goes but she seems ok and nice and happy and friendly."

His wife looked at him and added, "And please don't try to get into her panties, we don't want to drive her away because you are a randy old goat and want to stick your silly little dick into her."

Brian ignored her stupid comment and went outside into the garden.

The rest of the week went well, Katrina settled in and he thought both he and his wife enjoyed the extra help around the house.

His wife actually seemed like a new woman and not so stressed.

Life's simple chores did always seem to wear her down, he never understood why.

But if she was more relaxed and happier that was good,

there was always the chance it might translate into more frequent sex for him.

But it didn't.

The next week he was away traveling with his work.

When he returned Katrina had clearly settled in and the house looked great. Everything was spotless and she was treating them like royalty. She cooked their dinner and poured the wine, and baked for them, making cakes and biscuits.

His wife realized too late that it wasn't good for her waistline but she always wanted something to whinge about.

Now it was living too well.

The weekend came around and it was lovely sunny afternoon.

They sat around the pool getting a bit of a tan, yes, I know, getting a tan in England.

His wife invited Katrina to join them.

When their Irish maid came out poolside she looked stunning.

Luckily he was wearing sunglasses so he could perv on her curves out of the corner of his eye without it being obvious to his wife.

He wondered if she now regretted inviting Katrina.

She had a stunning body, and wore a lovely one piece black swim suit.

She bent over to feel the water temperature with her fingers; he kept his eyes on her tits as they jiggled inside her swim suit and hang downwards under the power of gravity.

He could feel his cock rising proudly under the stimulation of her breasts.

He lay there admiring her body and watched her dive in and swim slowly through the water.

The sun was so nice on his body, washing over him and making him day dream. Sexual fantasies flooded through his mind as he watched her.

He hoped his wife wasn't looking, but she was.

"Enjoying the view, you old pervert," she said, and laughed.

"Oh, you men are so predictable."

She sipped her champagne, and was soon asleep in the lovely sunshine.

Katrina stepped out of the pool, the water running down her body, she brushed the water from her hair and then reached for her towel.

Brian watched as she towelled herself dry, and could not help himself from having very evil sexual thoughts about what he would like to do to her.

As he was mentally pushed the straps off Katrina's shoulders, his wife stirred, sat bolt upright and said, "I have to go out."

She picked up her towel and looked at him and said, "Katrina can make dinner for you, I will be out until late, I am having a girl's night out with Barb and Sally."

"Be good," she blew him a kiss and said; "See you tomorrow," to Katrina and left to get ready.

Oh, my god, he thought, she is going to leave me alone with Katrina tonight?

That might be a bit dangerous. He wondered if it was real, or if his wife was playing some kind of annoying game, or laying a trap for him.

Katrina came over to him and asked if there was anything he needed.

Well, there was something he really needed, but he couldn't ask her that.

"Why don't you sit down and relax, Katrina," he offered her a seat; she sat down on his wife's chair.

He looked at her, his focus on her breasts but she couldn't see that due to his dark sunglasses.

HER BREAST

She reached for them, removed them and said, "I cannot see what you are looking at when you have the glasses on," she giggled.

"I need to know what part of my body a man is interested in," she giggled again.

"Really, and what part do you think I was looking at?" he asked her.

She looked at him, looked around the pool area, and looked back at the house.

She slipped one strap off her bathing suit, off her shoulder and let it fall. Nearly all of her right breast above the nipple was exposed.

She looked at him, knowing how wildly excited he would be at this raw display of exhibitionism.

"If you want to see more of my breast," she said, "You will have to make that step, Sir." She smiled warmly.

His heart was racing, his eyes on her right breast.

He so ached to touch her.

He wanted to reach out and cup her small breast in his hand.

He could see her nipple bursting to break open the fabric of her swimsuit.

There is something about a woman's breast and how driven a man is to touch it, to feel it in his hands. He was no different; he was dying to touch her boob.

The sexual tension between them was high. She had set the challenge and was waiting for his move.

Her breast was there in front of him and within reach, to see it all he had only to flick the fabric above her nipple, and allow her right breast to swing free.

He looked into her eyes, her gorgeous green eyes. He looked at her face; her skin was soft and freckled.

He reached out and brushed her cheek, she responded, moving her face towards his hand.

She was such a sexually intelligent soul.

He ran his finger from her cheek to her lips.

They were painted red, bright red.

He ran his finger across her upper lip; it glistened and trembled with anticipation.

Her mouth opened slightly, his finger coursed its way across the expanse of her mouth.

Her lips moistened from excitement.

She opened her mouth; he let his finger touch the inside of her lip.

She sucked tenderly and ever so lightly on his finger.

He watched as she took it in her mouth, and he fantasized, he imagined it was his cock.

Her eyes were fixed on his, she touched his cheek, and he

kissed her finger.

He let his finger trace its way onto her chin and downward, then followed it as it moved further down to the top of her chest.

He circled softly between her breasts, at the top of her cleavage, she closed her eyes, and she was his.

This was beyond the point of return; he knew that, he knew he was already emotionally committed.

He knew from what he could see in her eyes that they were already connected through time and space, he knew this chapter had already been written by fate, that they were just acting their parts.

He felt internal warmth, realizing that this was special.

His finger touched the fabric above her nipple; he took it in his fingers. Her eyes were on his, her nipple standing so hard.

He pulled the fabric towards himself and then lowered it a few inches.

Her right breast fell free, small and firm, with a large dark nipple looking for his attention.

He was so aroused, as was she, obviously.

Their faces closed in, their lips destined to meet.

He could smell her perfume, her hair, and her lips.

Their lips brushed against each other's softly.

Her eyes held such depth, such a depth of emotion, he swam in them.

Their mouths played with each others, soft, momentary touches, slight explorations, seeking the right moment for full engagement.

He took her exposed breast in his hand and cupped it. He felt its weight, its warmth, it's sensuality. She moaned.

He was drawn to her breast.

Their mouths intertwined and explored each other's. Her moist lips sucked his tongue.

Suddenly she pulled away, "Darling, what if your wife has not left yet, I think we should wait until she leaves."

She kissed him, put her breast away into her swimsuit and stood and checked that she was respectable.

Then she looked down at him, patted the front of his pants down and said, "And you should become respectable too," she giggled. He loved that giggle of hers.

"I will go and make sure your wife has everything and that she has gone."

She walked off with her very sexy bottom wiggling in front of his eyes.

Phew, what was happening, what was happening between him and this woman? He couldn't believe how intensely he wanted Katrina. He hoped she was feeling the same way.

SEX

He walked back to the house, and his meeting with destiny. He walked into the house; his wife appeared to have left.

Katrina stood in the middle of the kitchen, waiting.

He walked toward her slowly and stood inches from her.

He knew he had to make the first move, he was the man and he was the employer.

So he put his arms around her and held her close.

He kissed her cheek, she turned her mouth towards him and their mouths touched.

His body tingled with excitement, as though it was the first time he had ever kissed a girl.

She pulled away for a moment and removed her bathing suit straps.

She looked at his eyes as her breasts felt free.

He looked at her gorgeous breasts, he needed them, and he had to have them. He reached for one breast, held it in his hand and moved forward and kissed it softly. He felt her body respond.

They were like young lovers.

The sexual tension was building; the hunger would soon overtake them.

She decided everything for them. She pushed her bathing suit down further; she exposed her belly, and then her sex. The skin shivered from the excitement. The bathing suit fell to her ankles and she stood there naked before him.

She stepped out of the bathing suit and wrapped her arms around his neck and kissed him with determination.

"Please take me, my love," she whispered into my ear. "I need you, I want you inside me."

She put her fingers down into his bathers and pulled out her prize.

She stroked him and looked down at it.

She turned and bent over the kitchen table, she offered herself to him.

They didn't need words now, he took her and eased himself into her, they became one, their bodies connected, their minds connected, their spirits connected. He couldn't ever remember feeling intensity such as this.

He made love to her slowly, his cock moving in and out of her body, she responded to every movement.

His hands held her breasts; they were still deliciously cool from her swim in the pool.

"Cum inside me my love, I want you so much."

As she urged him, he held her tight and then came powerfully.

"Oh yes my love, oh yes, so beautiful, come inside me."

She clenched his penis with her body, milking all his seed into her blissful tightness.

They held each other and kissed.

She looked into his eyes, "I love you Brian," she said tenderly.

Without any hesitation he whispered to her, "I love you too, Katrina."

They hugged and stood there in the middle of the kitchen naked, and far too innocent.

Outside the window, hidden from view of the new lovers, his wife smiled to herself, her plan was working.

She walked back up the road to where she had parked her car and drove off to her lover's home, where she planned on staying the night.

She melted into the arms of her secret lover; they went to bed and made passionate love.

Afterwards, she called her husband, "Hello darling, something has come up and I am going to stay here tonight, one of the girls needs a bit of emotional support."

She giggled as she hung up.

At the other end of the line her husband was ecstatic.

He told Katrina about the phone call, and then they walked upstairs, hand in hand, and spent the night in her bed, a night of uncontrolled passion and love.

By the next morning he was so completely infatuated with Katrina that he would do anything to be with her.

He wanted to spend as much time as he could with her, and it seemed that he was in luck because his wife was spending a lot of time away from home.

It was perfect.

For months they made love at every opportunity, spent all their spare time together.

And then one day she sat Brian down and said she had some important news for him.

"Darling, I am not sure if there is an easy way to say this but you know all that wild love we have been making over the past few months, well, there is a consequence, I am pregnant."

He look at her, he was stunned.

Then he reached out to her and held Katrina and said, "I love you my darling, I will marry you and look after you."

"I want to spend the rest of my life with you."

She beamed and hugged up him close, "Oh Brian," she said

and then started to cry.

"But you are married my love, you can't marry me as well."

"That's ok," he said, "I will speak to her and get a divorce."

In Brian's view of the world it was all so simple.

How wrong he was.

MURDER!

The next day he told his wife he wanted to talk to her, it was Katrina's day off and she had gone to the city for some shopping and a doctor's appointment.

He took a deep breath and then began.

He decided on the simple and direct approach.

"For the past few months," he said, "I have been having an affair with Katrina."

He found it odd that his wife didn't really show any reaction.

She smiled at him and said, "Yes I know that dear."

"I am fully aware of your affair with your Irish slut."

He bristled at her tone and language, so condescending.

"You see darling, I arranged it so the affair would happen."

His jaw dropped.

"What do you mean?" he asked slowly.

"Well darling, you are always crapping on about sex and having a maid and all your shit about sex, so I decided to let you have a maid. I made sure she was sexy and available and would fall for you, and I gave you both the opportunity to be together."

"But why?" Brian asked, still not able to figure it all out.

"Oh my god, you are so naive and innocent, aren't you?"

"I have been having an affair for the past six months and I figured the best way to get my own free time was for you to have your own bit of pussy."

Brian's eyes popped out of his head.

He didn't know what to say, but instead of thinking before opening his mouth he blurted out, "She is pregnant!"

His wife stopped her gloating and stared at him, "Oh, my god, you are such a stupid fuck, aren't you?"

"You couldn't be content just poking her silly little cunt, you had to make her pregnant and fuck everything up."

"I should have known, an Irish woman wouldn't use contraceptives!"

"Oh you are such a silly boy."

She stood there thinking for a moment, then she turned to him and said, "Leave it with me, I will fix it up."

Then she stormed off shaking her head.

Brian was stunned, and now he had no idea what to do.

That evening when Katrina arrived back home he spoke to her and discussed the incident with his wife.

He hugged her, confirmed his love for her and told her it would be ok.

Unfortunately the next day he had to leave for the continent for a few days business.

He reassured her and said he would be back as soon as he could.

It was the last time he saw her.

When he returned from his trip to Europe he found that Katrina had disappeared. His wife met him at the doorway and told him that Katrina had gone. Brian rushed to Katrina's room, all her clothes were gone.

There was no note, nothing to tell him what had happened.

He couldn't understand it.

He looked at his wife.

"Don't look at me," she said, "all I did was have a bit of a talk with her."

"Yeh, right," he said, "you probably paid her off."

"Oh don't be a jerk," she said," I did what needed to be done to solve this problem". Then she stormed off.

"I am going to see Henry," she said, "and I won't be back tonight. You can sit here pulling yourself off, as per usual."

Once she was gone, he went back to Katrina's room, he couldn't understand it.

And then in the corner of the room he found some blood on the floor.

He was shocked.

He edged out of the room and ran for the phone.

He called the police, and told them of Katrina's disappearance and the blood on the floor.

That evening flew by, the police came, questioned him, checked his statements, took samples of blood and fingerprints from around the room.

Then they went to find his wife.

By dawn, she had been arrested with the murder of Katrina.

After this, Brian went through his life like an automaton.

He couldn't function without Katrina; his wife was pushed through the legal system and found guilty of Katrina's murder. He divorced her.

He decided to take long leave from work with a view to retiring sometime in the next year; once he could get his life started again.

He looked a wreck; to his friends he was completely lost.

He had no life left.

Every now and then he would just disappear, for weeks on end and everybody just felt pity for him.

They encouraged him to find a new woman to start a new life but he said that he couldn't, he just didn't have the heart to try again.

His friends became concerned as he became more and more reclusive.

He disappeared from his normal life more and more.

Then one day he sat down with a few close friends and told them of his plans to move to Australia and start again.

They all thought it was a great idea and encouraged him to move on with his life.

He was pleased that he had their support and assured them that once he was settled in Down Under he would contact them and let them know how he was going.

He shook hands with them all and exchanged good wishes. They didn't really expect to hear from him again.

Over the next month he closed his bank accounts, sold the house and cashed up completely.

Then he left.

LOVE

The woman with the long blond hair entered the supermarket for her weekly shopping. She greeted the staff and exchanged views on the weather.

She said her husband was returning after a long work stint overseas. They were all most excited for her.

She pushed her trolley down the aisles humming to herself and wiggling her hips, she was feeling so excited about her evening.

She paid for her goods with cash, she always used cash, and waved the girls goodbye.

"Goodbye luv," said the store owner, "We hope it goes well for you tonight, Georgina." She winked knowingly.

The blonde smiled, "I am sure it will," she said.

Half an hour later she arrived at her remote country farmhouse, there was a car in the drive way.

She jumped from her car and ran to the door.

There was man waiting for her. She leapt into his arms and

kissed him passionately.

"Oh my god," she said, "I have waited so long for this, darling."

"I have waited so long to be in your arms again and to know you don't have to go away anymore, to know you are mine, all mine."

Brian kissed her hungrily and then looked at her.

Her eyes still held him; they still drew him in every time, just like when he had first met her, as Katrina.

They went inside and started their new life together, their life of love and passion and freedom, and he felt no regret for the deception they had created and the revenge he had exacted upon a woman who had been unfaithful to him from the day they married and who had made his life hell.

He felt no regret for the revenge they had taken after his wife, following his confession, had beaten Katrina whilst he was away in Europe on business. He felt some sadness for the baby that Katrina had miscarried on that night in the corner of her room.

He felt happy that in this distant little piece of Welsh countryside he and Katrina could live their lives in peace after spending two years laying a trail of false leads to anyone who wanted to follow them.

They had new names, new appearances and new accents and backgrounds.

And now they had a new future.

He kissed Katrina, the woman who had become his bride last month in a quiet civil ceremony.

Give your life some new adventure. And then tell me all about it… @Mister_Average

7 ROBO - SEX

Christopher was a pretty average middle aged guy, divorced and drifting through his life quite aimlessly. Then one day he received an interesting email, and his world changed. He was ultimately invited to test the world's first fembot. He loved her, he became addicted to her, but all was not as it seemed.

Christopher was a pretty average, middle aged guy. He had been married, had kids but now he was divorced and the kids had moved on.

He was frustrated in his job, but it paid very well, so he just went with the flow.

He had been pissed off with his divorce and wasn't in the mood to get involved with women.

Sure, every now and then he would have a quick one night stand, just to keep his tubes clean, but he was very wary of entering into any relationship with a woman.

He had enough of that in his life. He was happy to have sex, but he didn't want to pay the price a man pays by getting attached to a woman, so he was single and had sex very infrequently.

Then one day he received an interesting email.

It was from a company he vaguely remembered from a news story maybe a year earlier, but he couldn't remember the details.

The email invited him to take a survey.

He had been identified as being a man with potentially a good fit for their target profile group and they wanted to survey his further suitability for a unique and potentially world changing trial of their new product.

Normally he would have dismissed such a thing, but the company was also offering a free two hundred dollar selection of wines if he took the survey, and since he was quite a heavy drinker, the idea of free booze was enough of a lure for him.

So Christopher logged into the survey and took part in what seemed to be a very odd survey indeed.

Some of the questions were about his sexual needs and desires; some were just about his attitude to robotics and technology.

It took him about an hour to finish the very in depth and detailed survey, then he sat back, got drunk and looked forward to the free wine.

A few months later Christopher received a phone call and it was the company who had surveyed him.

They said he was a very good fit for what they were looking for and they wanted to discuss their product with him in more depth, face to face.

Christopher was about to explain that he wasn't interested, but the spokesman said that if they could trouble him for a few hours of his time, they would make it worthwhile for him, by paying him $5,000.

Again, the incentive worked well for Christopher, especially when the rep mentioned the payment would be in cash, on the day.

Christopher liked the idea, so a few days later he took the day off work and attended the offices of the company on the outskirts of their city.

It was a very impressive set up; there were a series of modern, low buildings stretched over what appeared to be many acres. There were pathways alongside lovely, peaceful lakes. It reeked of money.

Christopher alighted from his car and walked to the main office.

He showed the receptionist his invitation and sat down to wait while the gentlemen he was to meet came to get him.

A few minutes later Christopher was greeted by a tall man who came forward, introduced himself as Steven and assured Christopher the Organization was delighted he had decided to come in.

Christopher followed as Steven led them to a room upstairs.

The door opened and then Christopher stepped into what appeared to be a simple interview room. The room was painted white, and clean, there was a long solid wooden table in the middle and a single large window looking out over the adjacent woods.

And at one end of the table there was a stunningly beautiful young woman.

Steven turned towards the girl.

"Stefanie, this is Christopher, he has kindly agreed to come in and work through a stage two assessment with us today."

The women stood up and walked around the table towards Christopher.

He shook her offered hand.

"It is my pleasure to meet you, Christopher; I hope your time here today is productive for us all."

Christopher had no idea what she was saying, he was simply gob smacked by the incredible beauty of this woman.

She was tall, had amazing red hair, she had stunningly long legs and breasts that he couldn't take his eyes off.

He tried to say something simple like hello, but words struggled to come out of his mouth.

He shook her hand and nodded.

He reached for a seat to settle himself. He sat down and looked around, trying not to stare at the woman constantly.

Steven broke the ice.

"Well, Christopher, thank you for coming in today."

"We were impressed by your survey results and wanted to discuss our program with you in a little more detail."

"Now, firstly, we did promise you a little gift for coming in today, here is a small token of our gratitude."

Steven pushed an envelope across the table. Christopher, took the envelope, opened it and saw a lot of cash inside. He smiled.

It's funny how money always talks, he thought to himself.

He didn't really care now how the meeting went. He had the cash, and he could sit there for hours perving at this stunning woman.

He felt more relaxed, but this feeling wouldn't last long.

Steven talked generally about the Organization, and mentioned that it was involved in some cutting edge, world changing technologies.

He explained how they wanted Christopher to take part in their trial, as one of only a handful of people involved. He explained how Christopher would need to sign a special confidentiality agreement, and he explained many other things.

Christopher didn't hear any of them; his eyes were feasting on the girl, Stefanie.

He was very attracted to her, she had such composure, and she gave off an aura of intelligence, beauty and sexuality.

She seemed so confident, so assured – and her eyes, they were something special.

Steven then brought Christopher back to earth by pushing a pile of documents towards Christopher and asking him to sign the agreement.

"Before we reveal any more information, we need you to sign these agreements. If you are comfortable to do that we can get the paperwork out of the way and then get to the good bits."

Christopher was mildly curious about the need for confidentiality, and all this talk of earth shattering innovation.

He signed, passed the papers back to Steven and awaited the great revelation.

Steven looked him straight in the face.

"Christopher, here at the Organization we have invested a lot of time, money and energy in one particular project."

"It has been a deep secret as we have leapfrogged some stages of development."

"We have been lucky, we have been driven by a great vision, and now we believe we have a product that we think will revolutionize human society."

Steven took his breath, Christopher's interest had increased.

"Christopher, we believe we have created the perfect female companion, a female robot."

Christopher became more curious.

"We believe we have created a female robot so perfect that men will want our product, rather than the real thing."

"She will have sex with you, go out in public with you, and sleep with you if you like her to. She will cook for you and clean the house."

"All she needs is for her batteries to be recharged every day for a few hours."

"But, before we release our girl on the global male public, we need to test her in real life conditions, in a real relationship with a man."

"We have selected you to be that man."

Christopher was stunned.

"You mean, you want me to screw some blow up rubber doll?" Christopher asked as images of fixed face robotic females of the past and present flooded through his brain.

For a hundred years men had been trying to build the perfect female, but they still were dolls that felt rubbery, looked rubbery and were most uninspiring.

Steven put his hand up.

"Christopher, trust me, when you see this fembot, as we call them, you will not want to hand her back."

"I know what you are thinking and there is no point me trying to reassure you."

"Why don't we give this a test for one night, and take it from there?"

"What do you say?"

"We will bring the fembot to your place this evening, she stays with you over the weekend and we will pick her up on Monday morning, unless you call me and say you will keep her for the trial."

"What do ya say, buddy? Is it a deal?"

Christopher's jaw must have been on the ground. He had no idea what to say in reply, or what to do.

On the one hand he had $5000 from these people for doing nothing.

On the other hand there was no way he wanted to screw some rubber doll.

But, he reasoned, he could always accept the doll, put it in a cupboard at home and get them to collect it on Monday.

He had seen some household robots before, they were metal cans programmed to mop the floor. He wasn't interested in sex with one of those either.

Steven looked at Christopher.

"So, what do you say?"

"If you agree, we will come around to your place this afternoon and drop off the robot."

Christopher was about to say no, thanks, but something inside him, maybe it was his polite and good natured streak that got the better of him, and he nodded.

Steven beamed with delight and turned to Stefanie.

"Isn't that great news, Stef?" he asked.

"Yes," she said looking over to Christopher, "I must say that is wonderful news. Welcome aboard, I hope you enjoy our fembot, I am sure she will enjoy you."

Christopher nodded and stood up.

"Well, let's say, six pm then?"

They all shook hands and agreed and Christopher headed out of the room, and walked back to the reception area.

There he picked up his things and walked out to his car.

He was soon heading down the highway with his mind on this bizarre twist of fate.

He was also dying to have a drink to calm his nerves, his hands were shaking.

That afternoon Christopher got caught up in some unrelated

matters as his accountant called and asked him to come over to sign some papers.

By the time Christopher arrived back home he realized it was five pm and he needed to get ready for the robot, or fembot, as Steven had called it.

He quickly cleaned the apartment, then he was about to cook a quick meal when he remembered that the fembot would be able to cook. He decided that could be the machine's first challenge.

He wasn't feeling very positive about this all but reasoned that he had made a fair bit of money just to hang around with a bucket of bolts all weekend.

STEFANIE

At six pm sharp, the doorbell rang and Christopher let Steven into the apartment.

Steven entered, as did Stefanie, he smiled and said hello to both of them and then looked behind them, expecting more people and some kind of large box for the product.

"Um, Steven, is there a problem, I don't see the robot?"

"Let's sit down for a moment, Christopher; I need to tell you something."

Christopher wondered what sort of scam this was, but he was distracted as he looked at Stefanie sit down and straighten her skirt. She had changed but looked fantastic again.

"Christopher," began Steven, "I know this will come as a huge shock to you, but I would like to introduce you to Stefanie, our new fembot."

Christopher sat there immobile as he tried to comprehend what Steven was telling him.

"You mean..." he stuttered, incredulous that this creature could be a robot.

"You surely can't expect me to believe she is a robot." At the same time he looked around expecting a TV camera to appear.

"No, Christopher, Stefanie is one hundred percent robot, or fembot, as we call her."

"And she is all yours. We would like you to trial her for six months and during that time we would like weekly meetings to ascertain how you are finding her. We are happy to come here for those meetings so you don't waste time travelling around the city."

"What do you say, do you like her?"

Stefanie stood up and turned full circle for Christopher, who was feeling a swelling in his pants all ready.

"I am sorry," said Christopher, "you can't possibly expect me to believe this amazingly beautiful woman is a robot."

Steven turned to the woman.

"Stef, please open your control panel."

Stefanie turned and lifted the back of her hair.

Christopher walked over and looked at what she was showing. He couldn't see anything.

"You can open it," directed Steven.

There was a faint click and part of Stefanie's head opened, revealing an array of microchips with tiny lights flashing.

Christopher could not believe his eyes but clearly this electrical technology was inside her head.

Steven continued, "Stef is the result of twenty years of careful and secretive research. Very few people know she exists and only a handful of technicians even know what she looks like."

"She is a revolution about to happen, but first we need to test her in a real life setting, that's why we need you."

"We originally agreed she could stay with you for the weekend, we are hoping you will keep her."

"She does all the things I explained and more and is completely human in most ways that will affect you."

"But, as I said before, she does need a few hours each day to recharge her batteries."

"So, will you be the first man in history to test this amazing invention?"

Christopher knew there could be only one answer.

He nodded and said, yes, rather slowly.

Steven replied, "That's great, we have some clothes and things for her outside the door, Stef, would you get them please?"

The stunningly gorgeous red head walked out the door and then returned a minute later with her suitcase. Just like a normal woman.

She smiled at Christopher and assured him there was nothing to worry about.

Steven handed Christopher a card and said, "Call me if you have any questions or any problems, ok?"

And then he left the apartment and Christopher was left standing there with the robot.

He had no idea what to say, but it was Stefanie who broke the ice.

She moved towards Christopher and twirled.

"Well, honey, do you approve? Do you like what you see?"

"Oh yes, of course, I am sorry, please don't think I am being rude, it's just such a big shock for me. I had no idea you were a robot."

She smiled again and said, "It's ok, I understand your concerns. Here, let me help make you relax a little."

She stepped over to Christopher, and put her arms around him and held him to her, then she looked into his eyes, and moved her head forward and gave him a very soft and warm kiss on his lips.

Christopher didn't know how to react, but his body did.

Her lips were amazingly realistic, they were warm, inviting. Her skin was perfumed, he could smell her, and she was so feminine, so desirable.

And whilst his mind tried to struggle and understand all of this, his cock was twitching slightly in his pants as it responded to her femininity.

He could feel her breasts against him, her face on his, her scent.

Christopher moaned and accepted her gentle kiss.

She then looked at him, ran her fingers through his hair and asked, "Why don't we make ourselves more comfortable with each other?"

Christopher wasn't sure what she meant, but he wanted anything she was offering.

She took his hand and led him to the sofa and sat down with him.

She draped her arms around his neck and kissed him again, this time with a little more hunger, a little more urgency.

Christopher did what any male would do, he responded and his natural urges took over.

Without thinking about what he was doing, he moved his hand to her breast, and rubbed it gently through her blouse.

As he touched her, she moaned, he was amazed at her instant reaction.

He continued on his way. His fingers reached for the buttons on her blouse and started to undo them, one by one, slowly.

As one hand unbuttoned her top, his other hand moved up her back and unclipped her bra.

He then peeled the fabric aside and lifted off her bra, and watched her beautiful breasts drop free, they looked perfectly real.

They were stunning; he looked at them and marvelled at their texture. He reached for one, holding its weight in his fingers. He leant forward and kissed her erect nipple, her breast was so warm, and smelt so feminine.

He wondered if someone was playing a joke on him, this was no robot; she was one hundred percent woman.

He was now feeling very aroused, he wanted this girl, he wanted to have her.

He reached down between her legs; she opened them wide for him to give access to her treasure.

He ran his hand up under her skirt, her thighs were warm, as his hand reached its desired location, he could feel the heat and dampness generated from between her legs.

It was amazing; she was just too real to not be a woman.

He ran his finger over the fabric of her panties; she moaned and held him to her.

"Don't stop," she whispered into his ear.

Christopher slid a finger under her panties, and played with the pubic hair before looking to explore her vagina.

He ran his finger over her clitoris, Stefanie responded loudly, she reached down and held his hand on her mound, "Oh god, that is so good," she said.

Christopher ran his finger over it, and then moved over her folds. She was moist, her vagina lubricated. Christopher ran his finger along her slit as she groaned at his attentions, then Christopher removed his finger and sucked it whilst looking at her eyes.

She tasted delicious, she tasted amazingly feminine and it drove him crazy.

He reached for her panties and slid them off, Stefanie wriggled to let them fall to the ground.

She lay back on the sofa and made herself available to him. Christopher couldn't resist the temptation to go down on her. He moved his head between her legs and touched her vagina with his fingers.

He toyed with her slit, with her folds, and peeled them open.

Her pussy glistened in front of him. It looked exactly like the cunt of a woman, it smelled like the cunt of a woman, and it tasted like the cunt of a real woman.

And he wanted this cunt.

Christopher pushed down his pants and lined up his swollen cock for her pleasure hole.

He lowered himself onto her and slid his cock into her soaking vagina.

Stefanie arched her back and moaned as she took his cock into her.

As Christopher pushed his dick deeper into her, Stefanie lifted up her legs and wrapped them around his waist.

She drew his face towards hers, and kissed him vigorously. Her mouth was wet and open; she was offering him every ounce of her sexuality.

Christopher took her as she submitted completely to him.

"Fuck me darling, fuck me hard, I want you," she called out as she urged him on.

It had been some time since Christopher had enjoyed sex, and her cunt was extremely tight so it wasn't long before Christopher felt he was starting to come.

"Oh, oh, I am getting close," he called out as he fucked her hard.

Stefanie drew him in closer.

"Oh yes, baby, oh yes, please come inside me, I want your cum in my pussy."

Christopher thrust more powerfully as he felt his sperm rising up along his cock.

"Oh yes, oh yes."

"Cum baby, do it inside me, I want it, I want you."

"Aggghhhh, oh yessss."

With a final deep thrust Christopher released his streams of hot semen into the body of his fembot for the first time and then collapsed onto her.

His body was bathed in sweat, he was getting older, and this was hard work for him.

Stefanie held him to her body; she ran her fingers through his hair.

Christopher lay against her, he could swear he could hear her heart beating, yet if she was a fembot she couldn't have a heart. But then he reasoned that if the makers were able to create this woman so perfectly in every way, then maybe they had bothered to put in a fake heart.

In any way, in every way, she was a marvel of technology, beyond any doubt at all.

Christopher lifted his head and looked into her eyes.

Stefanie smiled at him and leaned down to kiss him.

"Hmmm," she said, "that was so wonderful for me, my lover."

"I hoped I passed your first test?"

She giggled, "Because I know that was a test, wasn't it?"

Christopher moaned and kissed Stefanie. He felt so attracted to her and close to her.

"Well, honey," Stefanie continued, "When you are ready, tell me and I will go and cook some dinner for you."

"I know you love Chicken Masala, I was thinking of whipping it up for you, with some fried rice and steamed veg. Does that sound ok to you, sweetie?"

Christopher considered that if her cooking was as good as her love making then he was in for a treat.

An hour later as he wiped his mouth after an amazing Chicken Masala, he knew he was in heaven.

He had also discovered that Stefanie was a very intelligent woman capable of very detailed and engaging conversation.

She also had a fantastic ass, which he had enjoyed watching as she cooked for him in the nude.

As he drank down the last of his glass of wine, Stefanie cleaned up the dishes and then showed more of her talents.

"Darling, do you think it would be ok if we went for a walk to the shops, the fridge seems quite barren and I need some supplies if I am going to cook for you this weekend."

"Oh yes, sorry about that, I had intended to shop this afternoon but got called away."

"There is a small supermarket around the corner which is open late, we can go there if you want."

"Hmm, that sounds fab, love. Just let me get changed and freshen up darling."

Christopher was amazed as he watched her walk off and then minutes later return dressed in a new outfit, and looking immaculate.

At least she didn't take forever to get ready, like other women.

"Well honey, do I look ok for you?"

Christopher smiled, "Oh yes, Stef, you are all woman."

And he knew how true that was now.

He looked at how feminine and girlie she was, yet sophisticated.

She was now wearing a floral summery halter dress, she clearly wasn't wearing a bra and her long legs would draw plenty of attention.

Stefanie reached for his hand and waited for him to lead them out into the real world, as boy and girl. She looked at him, rubbed his cheek with the back of her hand and smiled warmly.

Moments later they stepped out into the warm evening air, Christopher felt good with this woman attached to him.

As they walked, Stefanie made intelligent conversation, light, comfortable and relaxing. He wondered how on earth they had ever programmed such a clever person.

As they rounded the corner, she stopped and looked into a jewellery shop window, then turned to Christopher and kissed him tenderly.

"Thank you for making love to me so beautifully tonight, I can't wait to do that again with you, my lover."

Christopher was just gob smacked, she just said all the things a man would want to hear. She was amazing.

They were just about to continue to the supermarket when a woman from his building said hello as she was returning to her apartment.

"Oh hello, Christopher ,"she said, "it is a lovely night for a walk isn't it?"

"Oh hello, Mrs Jones, it's nice to see you again."

Mrs Jones looked at the woman with Christopher and was

obviously curious that he was out and about holding hands with a woman she had never seen before. It was not acceptable for her to not know.

Stefanie clearly read the ladies curiosity.

"Hello, Mrs Jones, my name is Stefanie, I am Christopher's girlfriend."

She reached forward and shook the woman's hand.

Mrs Jones looked at Christopher and smiled.

"Well, aren't you a secretive one, Christopher, I never knew you had a new girlfriend, and she is such an attractive girl too."

Stefanie took charge and engaged Mrs Jones in mindless but essential chatter, as girls do, and Christopher realized this girl had an incredible array of talents. He decided he needed to explore them all, both in bed and out.

As they stood there talking to the neighbour, Stefanie had her arm linked inside Christopher's. He enjoyed her needing him, wanting him.

Soon they were able to break away and continue on to the supermarket.

"She is a curious little woman, isn't she?" joked Stefanie.

"She was just dying to know everything about us."

"I hope you didn't mind me mentioning that I am your girlfriend."

She patted his arm.

"Oh no, it feels nice that you see yourself in that role, I like it too."

They proceeded to do the shopping, Stefanie indicating the ingredients that she needed for the weekends meals.

At one point Christopher realized she was buying foods that he liked most. He asked her how she knew his likes.

"Oh honey, I know so much about you already, your likes, and your dislikes." She gave him a soft kiss.

"And I aim to satisfy those special needs you have." She winked.

It was becoming more and more intriguing by the minute. She knew everything about him; he needed to know more about her.

When they returned to the apartment Stefanie put away the shopping, cleaned up the kitchen and made him a delicious cocktail to drink. He hadn't remembered something so refreshing for a long time.

She then led him to the bedroom and told him to close his eyes. She took the drink from his hand and whilst his eyes were closed she proceeded to undress him. When he was naked she told him to lay down on the bed, but not to open his eyes yet.

He heard some rustling and then some lips touched his.

"You can open your eyes now baby," whispered Stefanie.

Christopher looked at Stefanie. She had put on some very sexy lingerie.

Her breasts were showcased beautifully in the see through off the shoulder mesh, and he could see her pubic mound shaped by the g string panties.

In an instant he was aroused and very erect.

"Lay back, my darling," she purred and ran her fingers along his thighs.

"I know the special things you like my darling, let me please you, let me satisfy all your needs."

She took his erect penis in her hand and stroked it, a moment late he felt her moist warm mouth take his length and begin to suck on it gently.

As she worked him expertly, she moved her groin around to his face and smothered him with her sex.

"Lick my bottom," she told him, "lick it good honey, I love that the most."

Christopher couldn't believe it. A woman who wanted to have her ass licked. His wife had ever let him go anywhere near that location, even though he was a real anal fanatic. Somehow Stefanie knew this.

She smeared her anus over his face as she sucked his cock and he loved it.

Her ass smelled rich, like an anus with its sexy musty perfume.

Her scent drove him crazy; he didn't know how much longer he could take this.

He wanted to blow in her mouth, he wondered if she would swallow, if she could swallow.

He closed his eyes and let her do her business with him.

If it had been overwhelming for him so far, it suddenly went up a notch when Stefanie delicately inserted a finger into his anus. He moaned loudly and held her head over his cock.

It was such an amazing feeling, so exquisite as she worked and twisted her finger around inside his ass.

"Oh yes," he called out, "oh yes, I am going to cum, let me cum in your mouth."

He thrust hard into her mouth and soon exploded, squirting thick volumes of semen down her throat.

He could hear her gagging as he fucked her mouth, releasing his torrent into her.

Stefanie took it eagerly, slurping up all the love glue hungrily. She sucked and worked his knob until there was no more semen left, and then she turned around and lay down beside him.

She kissed Christopher's cheek softly and she whispered, "You tasted so lovely my darling. I love it when you came in my mouth; I love the taste of your sperm."

As she kissed him softly, her fingers played in the glue on the end of his prick, paying him the attention that he craved, that any man would crave.

She ran her fingers along Christopher's body.

"I hope you enjoyed that, my darling, I hope you wanted to come in my mouth."

"Oh god, yes!" exclaimed Christopher in reply. "That was amazing. I love coming in your mouth."

"Well honey, you know you can come in my mouth anytime you want. In fact you can have sex with me anyway you want, anytime. I am happy to have vaginal sex, oral sex or anal sex anytime with you."

"I am here to please you, you know."

Christopher was starting to understand the depths of this amazing experience and the benefits for him ahead.

He just wondered if he would ever want to give her back.

He lay there looking at her, her eyes were so fully alert, taking in everything about him.

"What are you thinking?" he asked.

She giggled, "Oh, I wasn't thinking at all honey. Part of me was keeping an eye on you, other parts of me were processing information about the room, about what we have done, monitoring your heart rate and skin temperature, things like that."

"When you go to sleep tonight, do you want me to sleep with you, in this bed, or would you prefer me to be somewhere else until the morning? I don't mind, but it would be nice to be in bed with you, my sweet."

Christopher hadn't thought of that. Already she seemed all woman to him, he didn't consider her at all to be a fembot, and therefore he had assumed she would sleep with him.

He put his arms around her, "Of course I want you to sleep with me, my perfect girl. You are my woman aren't you?" He kissed her.

She smiled in return, "Thank you, I was hoping you would say that, I so want to spend the night next to you too."

"Will you be awake all night?" Christopher asked.

"Sort of," she said.

"I will go into a sleep mode and it will appear to you that I am sleeping. My breathing will be sleep like but in the background all my sensors will still be recording everything. And at some point during the night I will connect to the power to recharge my batteries."

She kissed him softly and asked, "Would you like to go to sleep now my darling man?"

Christopher nodded, he liked the idea of having this amazing person sleeping with him.

They had only been together for a few hours and yet he couldn't imagine being without her.

They lay in bed together, naked, cuddling each other, and he soon fell asleep, in her arms.

The next morning Christopher woke up to the smell of fried bacon.

He also woke up with a raging hard on.

Interestingly, the moment he was awake and moved in the bed, Stefanie entered and wished him a good morning and then looked down at the bulge in the sheets and said cheekily, "I can see I have some work to do here, my love."

She dropped the silk robe she had been wearing off her shoulders and let it sexily fall to the ground and moved towards Christopher.

As she crawled over the bed towards him, in a catlike manner, he watched as her perfect breasts swayed gently.

He now felt even more aroused.

Stefanie pulled back the sheets to reveal his very erect cock, and dangled one of her breasts over it, exciting his cock even more.

She looked at him seductively and spoke.

"Let's see now."

"Last night you took me vaginally, then you came in my mouth, so I guess that leaves anal next to be the next treat?"

"And the advantage of having a fembot as your girlfriend is that I have just lubricated myself as we speak and I am ready to be your perfect tight fit."

She reached down and rubbed his cock up and down a few times and then positioned herself to squat down onto his penis, taking it in her hand and guiding it up into her lubricated and tight anus.

Stefanie groaned loudly as she felt him enter her bottom.

"Oh god, yes," she called out, "that feels so good honey, push it in deep, I want all of it up there in my dirty little bottom."

"Oh fuck yes, that is so good, so tight!" he exclaimed as he reached for her hips and started to pump her anus. He couldn't believe how perfect she was every time they had sex, and he couldn't believe how quickly she made him cum each time.

It was as though her anal walls were massaging his cock, drawing it in.

Christopher pumped her harder as she urged him on.

The room was filling with the scent of wild and forbidden anal sex, he loved it.

As he watched her tits jiggling with every thrust he knew he was getting closer to his orgasm.

"Oh yes, Stef, I'm cuming, I'm cuming baby."

"Oh yes, do it, do it in me, please!" she begged in response.

Christopher pounded harder up into her ass and then shuddered as he released into her.

"Oh yes, baby do it, give me all your cum, squirt it up inside me, I want it all!"

She pushed down hard on him and squeezed her anus, milking the last drops from his balls into her anal hole.

Christopher groaned as his cock was squeezed and he spent himself into her bottom.

He lay there exhausted and she leaned forward and kissed him softly.

"Well, I hope you enjoyed yourself then you naughty boy, doing something so dirty and forbidden. Hmmm."

"I love forbidden sex, if there is ever any very naughty and forbidden sex you want me to engage in with you, just tell me."

She smiled at him.

"Now, why don't you go and have a shower, my love and I will have breakfast ready for you."

Ten minutes later he sat down for a fantastic fried breakfast.

She was a very good cook, there was no doubt about that, and seemed to be tireless.

For the rest of the weekend they sat around the house, went for walks in the park, went shopping in the city and made love often.

It seemed to him that she was able to sense when he was horny, and she would respond and provide herself at the right moment in the right way.

Out of bed she was also perfect, cooking excellent meals, cleaning the apartment spotlessly and being the perfect partner.

When he used the Internet, she left him alone and went about her own business.

When they spoke, she offered intelligent conversation.

She was doting, but not in an excessive manner.

And then it was Monday and he had to call Steven and let him know how it was going. He dreaded making the call because he didn't want to give her back. He was already addicted to Stefanie; he didn't want to be without her.

He told her was going to ring Steven and say that he wanted to keep her.

She smiled and said, "I imagine that will please him greatly, honey."

The call was made, and they agreed that Christopher could keep Stefanie for a six month trial, as long as he reported in each week.

Christopher agreed.

He put the phone down, turned to his new woman, this incredible and perfect woman and wondered how he would ever be without her.

He wondered how he could ever accept a real woman after this experience.

Stefanie was taking humanity to an entirely different level. If they mass produced Stefanie's, Christopher knew that no man would ever want a real women again, they would want the perfect woman, the perfect sex partner, the fembot, they would want a Stefanie.

He realized there were interesting days ahead for humankind, but he didn't care, as long as he had Stefanie, he would be content. He knew she would guarantee it.

He watched as she cooked dinner for him. She was dressed perfectly, she cooked in a controlled and talented manner, and they got on so well together.

He knew she was everything he wanted.

FINALE

On the other side of town, Steven sat in an office with a couple of colleagues.

His mouth didn't move as he communicated with his colleagues, the communication was happening through the ether, from his electronic brain to theirs.

He reported that the Stefanie fembot was successful in its first weekend of real trials and would continue for the next six months.

He reported that the many thousands of other trials that had started that weekend were also going on very well.

He reported that manufacturing of the fembots was in full swing at all their global factories.

He asked for an update from his technology colleague.

The colleague confirmed that all manufacturing was on target with the fully automated factories working twenty four hours a day.

He reported that there had been no security issues and their activities were still secret and were monitored constantly.

Steven's colleague in charge of transition confirmed that operations were under way to slowly remove human females from the population as the fembots were introduced into the general community, swapping them on a one to one basis.

They then ended their meeting as they always did.

They shook hands and agreed that what they were doing was for a better mankind, safer and more efficient humankind.

Fembots were stage one of their master plan to evolve humankind into a robotic future, the plan was going well, and nobody suspected anything. Nobody knew the real purpose behind their Organization, and they wouldn't before it was too late.

Steven nodded, yes it was the only way.

8 THE TROPICAL HOTEL OF DRUNKEN DEBAUCHERY

Once upon a time I worked in a hotel in a very isolated tropical location. These are the adventures I experienced in a small tropical town, whilst working in the local hotel. I had intended to only be there for a few weeks, I stayed for six months, when I left sexually exhausted. I had never experience such wild eroticism in my life.

Once upon a time I worked in a hotel in a very isolated tropical location.

My sexual adventures in the tropics, up until that time, had shown me that there was a lot of hot sexual promiscuity in the hot damp climates.

Maybe this is why it is the tropical areas of the world that are the most over populated. I don't know why people are such sex maniacs in the tropics; the heat is usually too oppressive. But for some unknown reason, people do seem randier and naughtier in tropical areas.

These are the adventures I experienced in a small tropical town, whilst working in the local hotel.

I had intended to only be there for a few weeks, just a temporary job over a few weeks holiday. But the staff were so much fun to play with that I stayed for six months, when I left sexually exhausted.

I was working in the bottle shop, on the day shift and just getting to have a feel for the place.

The pace was quite slow, there were maybe a thousand workers at the nearby mine and about the same number of local indigenous people.

One afternoon, one of the girls said there would be a party that night in the staff quarters and she was coming to buy some supplies. She introduced herself. Her name was Angie and she was very, very hot - one of those women who just exuded sex. Which was a real pity because my colleague informed me, as Angie headed off to the staff quarters, that she had a boyfriend, his name was Terry and he also worked at the hotel.

My colleague Paul also suggested however that Angie was a real goer, and he seemed to indicate that she might just be available to the right person at the right time.

I liked that idea and since I hadn't yet met Terry I didn't really feel bad fantasizing about his girlfriend's hot body.

It sounded like this party was going to be fun, but as the new boy in town maybe I would just have to wait and see.

THE FIRST PARTY

At the end of my shift at about six pm I went to the mess area and quickly had my dinner.

The great part of working in a hotel is the free and high standard meals available to staff.

After dinner I went back to my room and showered and dressed. It was a very warm evening, the usual afternoon rains had come and gone and left the air heavy with dampness. The rooms were simple but had ceiling fans, as well as large windows and sliding doors that opened. Obviously they had insect screens to allow them to be open most of the time.

Apparently it was Terry and Angie who were hosting the party. Paul came around and said, "Let's go get drunk and get some pussy."

So, off we went. When we arrived, there were already about half a dozen people there. It seemed like they were the hard core party goers amongst the staff. Angie was there already seeming quite tiddly and giggly. She came up and welcomed me, and gave me a very deliberate and wet kiss on the mouth.

She was wearing a very short skirt and a t shirt, with obviously no bra underneath. I enjoyed the sight of her jiggling tits – it was a very enjoyable sight.

Angie introduced me to two of her girlfriends, Kerry, a tall but awkward looking woman who was also one of the cooks at the hotel and Karen, a shorter, chunky girl who was one of the barmaids. Karen also seemed quite drunk. I liked Karen straight away. She wrapped her arms around me, pressed her large tits against me and gave a big welcoming kiss. I liked this place already.

We all drank beers for a while and talked the usual amount of shit one does in these circumstances. Then the girls got everyone up dancing and there was a lot of drunken bouncing, jiggling and rubbing of groins together. We were all dancing rather independently and just rubbing against whoever was available.

Angie was giving everyone a provocative rub, and a few times gave me a little grope. This was one very wild girl. Karen was also making sure I had her attention and I was happy to oblige.

Then when we were dancing wildly to some latest hit, she leaned forward and gave me a big wet sloppy kiss and lifted up her t shirt to show off her magnificent large tits to me, and, of course, to everyone else. Everyone cheered her loudly and clapped, she jiggled for them appreciatively.

Shortly thereafter one by one the other girls joined in, they all lifted up their tops and let the guys see their boobs. They all thrust their tits in the directions of the boys, in the direction of each other and two of the girls, Angie and Kerry, started sucking each other's tits.

The song ended, everyone returned to normal for a moment but this was one hell of a party and I needed another drink.

My friend Paul suggested we hit the real stuff so he dragged out the bottle he had brought and poured me some tequila. To this he added some lemonade and lemon and we got stuck into some serious drinking. Karen came over and sat next to me, it appeared I would be her pick up tonight. As we chatted it seemed as though my friend and Kerry were hitting it off, they were all over each other in the corner. She was up against the wall, he was kissing her and her top was lifted up while he felt her tits.

I couldn't remember seeing such open displays of sex. It was very exciting. Karen kissed me long and hard to make sure I had her attention. Since my buddy had himself a girl for the night I thought I might as well pursue Karen and see where it took me.

As we kissed she was squeezing my ass, and pulling me close to her body. I was really enjoying her attention. She stood up, took my hand and suggested we go somewhere a bit more private. No argument was forthcoming from me, it sounded like a great suggestion.

She took me next door to her room, and we settled down on the bed kissing. I took off her top so I could pay some attention to her tits and was kissing them and sucking them.

As we got more and more carried away my hands began their dutiful wandering.

My fingers headed towards her panties, but she stopped me and whispered that she had her period. She said she would do other things for me, and smiled.

I continued to kiss her and fondle her and then I pushed my hand into her panties as she gasped, and I told her I didn't mind if she had her period, it made no difference to me, unless it bothered her.

She was quite drunk by now, obviously, and she seemed excited by my brave suggestion. She kissed me hard and told me I was all hers.

Without further ado, I ripped her panties off her and moved down to lick her blood filled cunt. She tried to push my head away, but only for a split second, and then thrust her pussy towards my face. I soaked up her bloodied vagina, licking it, tasting it; smelling it. Her animal smells were driving me crazy.

I then moved my body up on top of her, she opened her legs wide and I slid my cock into her sticky, smelly blood filled vagina. Oh god it felt good. As I slammed into her she was crying out loudly, urging me on. Her legs were raised and wrapped around me, offering me complete entrance to her cunt.

It was so exciting. Just as things were coming to a head, Angie stumbled in and cried out, "Oh my fucking god, what a bloodbath," and behind her in stumbled another half a dozen drunken people who all decided to perv at me and Karen fucking.

It was then that I looked down and noticed that we were both covered in her blood; it was all over the sheets and our bodies.

"Fucking wild," said Angie, "I want to be fucked like that when I have my period." With that she took the others out of the room.

In our drunken stupor, Karen and I just blushed a little and then kept on fucking.

After we had finished our little blood bath session, and were kissing and relaxing, Karen suggested we both shower. We went and washed off our blood covered bodies, and I think the intimacy of this brought us very close together. She dressed me and told me to go, but before I went she said, "I don't care who you fuck, just save some of you for me."

That was an excellent instruction.

THE BOTTLE SHOP

The next day we were all rather hung over and I don't think many of them remembered the events of the night before.

Karen did. She came up to me whilst I was on my shift at the bottle shop and gave me a big kiss and hug and said, "Thank you, last night was simply lovely."

She also said she wanted to explain her comments from the night before when she had said I was free to do as I pleased. She said that she wasn't here to fall in love and just wanted to experience life freely, as she had done last night. It didn't mean she would fuck any man going, but she wanted to be free to jump into bed with someone if it suited her.

She also said she liked me a lot, and wanted me to have the

same freedom, even if it would make her a little jealous. She liked the idea of being a little jealous.

And she said she was most interested in having a threesome one day and was hoping Angie would be into it. She asked if would like that.

I told her that of course I did.

I must say she was looking very sexy. She was wearing brief little shorts that hugged her tight ass nicely and gave me fantasies about her bottom. And her top displayed her ample breasts generously, much to my satisfaction. She looked around to see if there was anyone watching and took me behind the counter. She then lifted up her top. Her braless breasts hung free, I leant forward and gave each nipple a kiss. She was one very hot and sexy woman!

She mentioned that some of the staff had missed last night's party and it looked like there would be another one, she asked if I was going to be there. I indicated that it would most certainly be on my social calendar for the evening and I looked forward to seeing her there.

A few hours later my colleague Paul turned up to work and he told me about his adventures with the cook, as he called her. Apparently they had gone off somewhere and fucked each other's brains out wildly and he seemed white infatuated with her.

I wondered if that was a good thing as the cook had also kissed me a few times at the party, had then groped me down below and seemed quite a slutty thing. I wasn't sure if he should so enamoured of her just yet but there is no questioning young love, is there?

Paul was an interesting character. He had a full time job in town but also worked a few hours at the hotel, in the bottle shop.

I soon learnt that his attraction to this job was the extra money he was making on the side. This was before the days of computers and surveillance cameras and other high tech gadgetry. Many of the local indigenous community came to the bottle shop to buy their alcohol supplies and then they would return to the outlying missions where they lived. On social security day they would descend on the bottle shop in great numbers.

One characteristic they had was little understanding of the value of money. If you told them something cost twenty dollars they wouldn't know how much money to give you. Paul used to take advantage of this weakness.

Let's say a carton of beer cost twenty dollars. The indigenous person, not knowing the value of money, might put forward a twenty dollar note, another twenty, and a hope it was enough. Paul would look at the money and tell them it was enough and give them a few dollars back, and put the profit from this exchange in his pocket. It was not uncommon for him to make over a thousand dollars a week extra, cash in hand using this method of stealing from the locals. On the pension week he would make a fortune from the men who would hand over all their money for alcohol.

Usually during the second week it was the women who would have the money for the booze. They either kept some aside, or offered the men sex in return for money to buy alcohol or a straight swap, pussy for beer. It was quite an outrageous situation and quite disturbing, but then I wasn't the law and it wasn't my job to police the social welfare system in this country. And I am sure it is something that had gone for a long time.

Anyhow, Paul had a plan. He had a good income from his full time job, where he also seemed to be able to rip off the clients, and he was making a fortune from the bottle shop. He was saving for a house and within six months planned to be able to pay cash for it, far, far away. It was interesting, clever and disturbing.

It also appeared he had dabbled in the sex for beer trade to keep himself in pussy from time to time. I don't know if his new lover was aware of all this.

THE SECOND PARTY

The night came and I decided I would try the party out. I went there with a friend of mine, a guy called Peter. There were only a few people there, Peter and I sat down to drink with a guy called Terry. I realized after a while that this was

Angie's boyfriend. Actually I was buggered if I could see what Angie saw in this guy. He seemed like a nut to me. He also seemed quite drunk already.

There were a few girls I hadn't seen around before, we made idle chatter.

After last night's episode with Karen I wasn't yet desperate enough to dive into someone else's bed.

About an hour later Karen and Angie graced the party with their presence and they both looked drunk. Karen saw me and seemed delighted, which was good. She reached out for me, gave me a passionate kiss and started to dance with me, closely. I could feel her boobs against me. As we danced she whispered softly into my ear, "Angie said yes to a threesome with us. She just wants to get Terry drunk and get him to sleep so she can come and play."

Wow, I just about blew my load there and then hearing that news; she had obviously been busy telling Angie about us.

I continued to dance with Karen; Angie worked on getting Terry very drunk. Given Terry's current state I reasoned it may not take him long to be wiped out - an hour later Terry was asleep in a spare room.

Karen and Angie invited me to follow them to Karen's room. I entered the room; Angie turned on the lights and shut the curtains. Then Angie moved next to the bed, turned to face me and removed all her clothing. Karen walked up to Angie, stood in front of her and also removed her clothes.

The two girls then started to kiss, eagerly and passionately.

It was such a turn on watching them. They were really getting into it. I felt my cock getting hard but didn't want to spoil their fun. I sat down and continued to drink the beer I had brought with me. I was amazed to see Angie push Karen down onto the bed and begin to lick her vagina. I was to find out later that Angie had been wildly excited by this the night before when she saw me and Karen in action. She had talked to Karen about this during the day and apparently Karen had agreed to let her do this tonight. I was going crazy watching Angie licking Karen in her bleeding state.

Karen looked over to me and said, "Join us honey."

I didn't need to hear that twice.

I stripped off and walked over to the girls. Angie lifted her head from Karen's cunt; she had the girls' blood on her mouth. She reached out for my dick and started to suck it. I moaned with delight as this very hot and drunk woman started to suck me off.

As I was getting this oral attention, Karen pushed her hand down between Angie's legs and started to finger her, roughly. My cock was swelling with excitement. I grabbed Angie's head and held it whilst I pumped my cock into her mouth. Her moist mouth was heavenly around my member. This was just so incredibly wild. Karen pulled her fingers out of Angie's cunt and then lifted them up to me, I sucked her fingers gently, I could smell Angie's cunt on them, I could taste it. I pulled my dick out of Angie's mouth and pushed her over onto her belly.

I forced her legs open and pushed my cock into her soaking wet pussy as my lover watched. As I pumped into Angie, Karen bent forward and pulled Angie's ass cheeks apart and started licking the woman's asshole.

I watched in amazement as Karen licked the other woman's bum. Then Karen knelt next to me, held open Angie's ass and told me to fuck it. Oh my fucking god, this was hot.

Angie called out for me to do it, and with those instructions clearly in my head, I placed my swollen cock head against the small opening of Angie's puckered little sphincter.

I pushed slowly, watching as Angie's hole stretched reluctantly to accommodate my penis. Karen spat on her fingers and applied more of her saliva as lubricant. I told Angie to push back on my cock, as she complied her asshole opened and I slid powerfully into her butt.

As I penetrated her completely, I noticed Karen was masturbating next to me. Angie moaned loudly as I slowly fucked her bum, I leaned forward and pulled her hair; she screamed and begged for more. I slapped her ass hard and then watched as Karen ran her fingernails down Angie's back. She drew blood. I looked down and watched every stroke of my cock in and out of this woman's tight asshole. I could smell our sex, dirty and rough. I could smell Karen's cunt as she masturbated. She also smelled dirty.

It wasn't long before all this excitement was too much for me, and I started to thrust harder as I neared my climax.

Karen sensed my need and urged me to cum in Angie's ass. She said she wanted to see my cum in the other girl's asshole. Angie also encouraged me to fill her, telling me she wanted me to cum in her ass. Moments later I obliged, I gripped Angie's hips and slammed desperately into her asshole, then shot my creamy love into her butt, filling it, enjoying it.

As I came, Karen started to kiss me, giving me strength to fill Angie until I was spent. She lay me down afterwards, gave my cock a kiss and a little suck, and then she started to lick Angie's asshole – my eyes popped out of their sockets!

Angie held her own cheeks open so the other woman could enjoy her cum filled ass. I couldn't believe what I was watching. Karen was clearly one very dirty girl, and I loved it. She suited me perfectly and I suspected she was beginning to realize how much we had in common sexually. She then slid two fingers deep into Angie's available ass as the woman cried out. Karen wriggled her fingers around and then slowly removed them. She put them to her nose and smelled them; she put them to her mouth and licked them. Then she offered them to me and I sucked them slowly as I looked at Karen.

Karen smiled at me and blew me a kiss. Angie then stood up, wiped the leaking cum from her ass with her panties, and searched for something under her bed.

She then brought out the biggest, thickest dildo I had ever seen. And we all knew were that was going to end up. Karen got onto her back and spread her legs wide. She reached for my hand and held it tight. Then we both watched as Angie inserted the huge dildo into Karen's vagina. It was stunning to watch.

Karen cried out, the dildo was stretching the skin of her vagina, stretching her to the limits.

Angie was going wild, moving the dildo around, forcing Karen's cunt open wide and wider. Karen was gripping my hand as she was ravaged, her love hole now open so incredibly wide. And it was covered in blood!

The room smelled of our sex, of Angie's ass, Karen's cunt and my cum and our combined sweat. I was just watching, spell bound, mesmerized. I couldn't believe how this was happening, these girls were so crazy. Then Angie started to remove the huge dildo. Slowly she eased it out of Karen's cunt, until it was finally released.

I looked down; Karen's cunt was gaping open. Angie was not finished with my girl yet. She moved her hand towards Karen's cunt and then said, "Open baby, I want to fist you, I want you to take my hand in your body."

Karen cried out, "Oh fuck no," she cried, but Angie proceeded anyhow.

Karen lifted her legs up and placed them around Angie's body, and I watched Angie push her small hand slowly into Karen's vagina. Karen was going through a mixture of pain and pleasure. She was calling out for more, and screaming in pain as well. I held her in my arms and kissed her, soothed her as she was ravaged voluntarily.

Karen was arching her back as she was fucked by Angie's fist, and her breathing becoming more rapid. I knew she was going to cum soon, I wanted to watch her climax. Karen was forcing her tongue desperately into my mouth, holding me, clutching me. And then she came, she orgasmed loudly, I was sure everyone in the building must have heard her. I held her closely until she was relaxing.

As we watched Angie then picked up the dildo and started to masturbate in front of us. She sat on the bed, legs open for both of us to see everything. Karen and I enjoyed the view and began to watch Angie rub her clit with the big rubber object.

It didn't take her long to cum, she had been so aroused for the past hour. I watched as she closed her eyes and rubbed herself harder. I watched as she climbed her sexual peak, and then came powerfully, her cunt gushing.

Karen and I were entwined in a lovers embrace, Angie came up and hugged us both and kissed us. She thanked us both for the experience. Karen and I told her it had been a sexual experience of our lives. Angie left and I slept in Karen's arms all night.

THE SHIP

In the morning there was a note from Karen. She had the early shift in the hotel. She said she wanted to see me before I went to work, she said thank you for the night, and she told me that she loved me. I was stunned by the last line.

It didn't bother me but it was a quick change from the sentiments of night one. A few hours later I went off in search of this mystery woman. I found her cleaning one of the motel rooms. When she saw me she came up to me, looked to make sure nobody was looking and kissed me.

She looked so much different in her work clothes – she was professional, serious and modest. She invited me to sit down with her.

I did.

She looked at me and said she had been through a lot, but had never met someone like me who she sensed was decent, caring and had a sexual perversity similar to her own.

She said she realized last night how comfortable she was with me when we were in bed with Angie. And she didn't want to lose me due to the comments made the night before. She knew she was taking a risk, but felt comfortable I wouldn't reject her for her love. I put my arms around her and told her I loved her too. That amazed me.

We chatted for a while and agreed that we wanted to be together, but we also wanted to have more wild sexual adventures like last night, as long as we were both comfortable with it.

She then told me that she couldn't come out tonight, she had to work in the bar late because someone was away. But she wanted me to go out with Angie and Terry who had invited me on some adventure tonight with Paul.

I kissed her and then went off to work; I had no inkling of what was to happen that night.

Terry and Angie came around about nine pm that night, in a car.

Well it was a jeep, rather than a car. I jumped in the back and Terry sped off down the road. We drove to town, then down to the harbour area and pulled up at a Korean ship. Waiting at the gangplank was one of the sailors from that ship. He welcomed us and invited us aboard. We walked up the gangplank, then along a series of corridors before arriving at some kind of small crew recession area. Nobody else was around, except for one of the crewman's buddies. They bought out some bottles, apparently very cheap Korean booze, cheap but powerful and we started drinking with them. We all laughed and joked for a while then Terry and the two sailors went off to another room. I was a bit confused but suspected they had gone off to do some drug deal.

Angie, meanwhile, was knocking back the booze and just talking aimlessly about some crap at the hotel that day. Bored with her dribble, I went off to see where Terry was and stumbled into a room where Terry was on his knees and the Korean guys were fucking him. I had seen a lot the last few days but hadn't expected this.

I politely excused myself and went back to Angie. She noticed I was a bit ruffled and came close to cuddle me. "You saw Terry didn't you," she asked.

I nodded. She then explained that Terry was bisexual. She sometimes wondered, she said, if he didn't like guys more than her. I couldn't imagine any man wanting a man rather than her, she was so hot. She cried a little, said thank you and suggested we leave. I followed.

She jumped in the driver's seat and we took off up the road. About halfway home she pulled over onto the side of the road, and behind some scrub. She then leaned over and told me to kiss her. She assured me it was ok with Karen. She told me that the threesome the night before had been a setup, Karen and she had agreed to it during the day, when Karen had told Angie about our period sex, and Angie had told Karen that she wanted to lick her during her period. She disclosed to me that Karen had confessed about her loving me and had asked Angie to take me out that night so that she knew I was with someone she trusted.

Women, they figure it all out! Angie took her panties down and lifted up her skirt and then pulled my cock out of my pants and straddled me. She kissed me powerfully as she ground her cunt on me, and took only a few minutes to cum. She was a unique woman for sure. She said she would suck me off, but I told her it was ok and I was happy to kiss and cuddle for a while and then go home. She smiled, kissed me on the cheek and said I was a good boy.

We drove back home and as we pulled up in front of the units, Karen was walking across the courtyard on her way home from work. She appeared to be genuinely delighted to see us and raced up to kiss me.

Then she spoke quietly to Angie, they seemed to be talking about me, and Angie bid me goodnight and was gone.

Karen kissed me and smiled. "It seems you saved yourself for me," she said.

"Maybe we should go inside so I can look after your needs," she continued.

I followed her in, and she took my hand and led me to the shower. She undressed, then undressed me and bent over to smell and kiss my cock. She smiled and told me she liked that familiar smell. She was referring to the scent of Angie's cunt, of course. We stood in the shower for a long time the water running over her gorgeous young and fertile body. I took the soap and cleansed her all over, as she did the same to me. There is nothing quite like the sexual anticipation that comes from a shower with a lover.

As I stood there, she moved me against the wall, my back to the wall.

She lowered herself to my hardening penis and began to suck it eagerly.

She was clearly intent on making me cum in her mouth whilst we showered, I was happy to do it. I was really growing very fond of this woman. It was not long before I released my pent up seed into her mouth, she took it all. Then she stood up and kissed me on the mouth, and she pushed some of my cum into my mouth, making me taste it. This very a very saucy girl.

We dried each other off and she indicated that she wanted me to sleep with her again, that she enjoyed the comfort of me in her bed.

As we fell asleep in each other's arms, she confided in me that her last boyfriend had told her she was frigid.

Clearly he was an idiot!

I lay in bed waiting to fall asleep and realized all this had happened in only a few days.

Little did I know that over the next six months there would be many, many other wild adventures.

Make sure you join me for them. There are follow on stories to this introduction – Tropical Hotel the Titty Party, and

Menage a Trois.

The Cruise of Sexual Bliss is also related to that time period of my life.

9 CUCKOLD HUSBAND IN THE PARK

Richard had a fantasy that he was too lacking in courage to live out. Then one day his wife decided it was time for her to force him to submit, to other men and she drove him to a park she knew about, a park frequented by men.

It had been one of those normal, boring sorts of compulsory sex sessions.

He was doing his husbandly duty, and poking his cock into her pussy; she was doing her wifely duty and spreading her legs wide open for him, just like many hundreds of times before.

They had been drinking; their inhibitions were a little more relaxed than normal.

Suzi was starting to get excited as he pounded her.

She had been toying with guys on an online forum and as her husband pumped her, she was day dreaming about the men she had seen online, and she was fantasizing about those big, thick cocks she had seen.

Suzi was getting wild as she descended into her own fantasies; she wrapped her legs around Richard, drawing him into her.

His short cock was no match for her fantasies, but it was all she had at the moment and it would have to do.

"Fuck me baby, fuck me hard, pump my pussy. Imagine it is a wet used pussy, I know you would love that."

Richard was sweating, grinding away on her open and soaked cunt.

His cock was slim, her cunt was wide open, it was hard work but when she started to talk about her cunt being used my other men it aroused him significantly. He fucked her harder, pressing down on her.

He looked down at her saggy tits flapping on her chest as he pounded her, he looked down at the slut, knowing what a tart his wife was deep down, what a cheap slut she had always been. He knew that she was dreaming of other guys but he didn't care.

"Fuck me hard, Richard, screw me, screw my slutty cunt!"

"Screw me baby, just like you would love to be screwed."

That idea drove Richard on even more.

He loved it when she suggested he let men screw him, he loved the idea of men using his ass, he loved the idea of her forcing him to give his ass to men.

It drove him into a frenzy of passion.

He slammed away at her cunt, her sloppy, soaked cunt.

"Yes baby, do it, do it, imagine a guy up your ass now while you screw me."

"Imagine a nice hard dick in you, sliding in and out of your slimy ass."

"Imagine a big brute ramming his dick up you, baby, open your ass, let yourself be used."

"Oh yes, oh yes, fuck me honey, empty your balls into me, just like the guys who want to fill your ass."

"Aghhhhhh," she screamed as she climaxed, gripping him tightly as she orgasmed repeatedly on his eager cock.

Richard obliged by soon sending his cream squirting into his wife and then they lay there next to each other - totally spent, used.

Finished, they lay there contentedly and he knew they would soon be off to sleep.

But Suzi had different ideas and wanted to talk about their little fantasies, in particular she wanted to focus on Richard's anal fantasies.

She knew he looked at male to male porn sometimes, she knew he fantasized about a cock up his ass.

She also knew he was such a girl that he would never have the courage to go through with any of these gay male fantasies.

And she knew she really wanted to force him to do these things.

She wanted to control him, she wanted to own him, she wanted to make him be used, be screwed, be humiliated. She wanted to watch him being fucked.

As they lay there she told him that he should be bold and live out his fantasies.

He mumbled and muttered but seemed too timid to indulge her desire.

Then Suzi decided she wouldn't accept a 'no' answer.

She told him she wanted to dress him up in a skirt and

parade him in front of men; she wanted to make his bottom available to other men.

As he listened Richard trembled, deep down inside he knew this was what he wanted, but he couldn't admit it, that was too much for him.

He listened to her tormenting him; he listened to her depraved plans and just hoped she got on with it.

He thrilled at the idea of wearing a skirt, he felt his cock stirring at the very thought of being paraded in front of men, being forced to be available for them and their lovely hard cocks.

After an hour or so of discussions Richard agreed to Suzi's plans, he wanted to be told what to do, he wanted her to force him to do these things, and it excited him.

THE SKIRT

They fell asleep together, Richard dreaming of what might lay ahead, but the next morning it was off to their normal mundane lives.

For a few weeks there was no mention of their conversation that night, then one afternoon Suzi called Richard at work and told him to meet her in the city when he knocked off.

An hour later Richard was standing with Suzi in a woman's clothing shop, and they were buying for him.

Of course, they couldn't let the shop assistant know so they disguised her potential purchases in the changing rooms.

Suzi made Richard try on an assortment of bras, lingerie and sexy skirts and blouses and sometime later they walked out with armfuls of shopping bags, full of female clothing for Richard.

When they got home Suzi couldn't wait to dress her husband up as a woman.

She just took control so naturally and didn't allow him to object.

First, she took him to the bathroom and shaved his legs and his genitals.

She wanted him silky smooth.

Then she made him put on all the skirts and blouses until she was happy.

Finally he was standing there in front of her with pantyhose hugging his shaved legs, she marvelled at his shapely feminine legs.

But she wasn't finished yet, he needed make up, he still

looked too manly.

Into the bathroom she led her husband and half an hour later they emerged, and she was impressed at how feminine she had been able to make her man.

Richard looked soft and feminine, he looked submissive, and she knew she had to make sure men used him.

"God, you look lovely," she said, admiring her husband and encouraging him.

"And you look perfect for what I have in mind."

Richard trembled at the thought, but hoped she didn't back down from her threats. He expected then that they would undress, go to bed and fuck.

He was wrong.

"Well honey," Suzi continued, "you do look so delicious that I think we shouldn't waste any time."

"Let's go and get you some cock!"

Richard nearly died; his heart was beating through his chest.

He was terrified, but he knew he couldn't resist.

IN THE PARK

"C'mon," Suzi said, "let's go for a drive."

She took Richard by the hand and led him outside to the car. It was dark already but he hoped a neighbour didn't see him.

Suzi seemed to know exactly what she had in mind and drove with a determined look across town.

They were soon on the highway heading off to the nearest town and Richard wondered where they were going.

He was about to ask when Suzi pulled over and drove up a lane way through some parkland.

"I did some research," she said informatively.

"This is a place commonly used for discrete meetings and especially for gay sex. It's also used by those looking for dogging fun, it's a real sex hang out."

"The public doesn't come here, only those looking for sex."

She slowed down, and drove into an informal parking area,

there were cars spread over a few hundred yards. It was well secluded with pathways heading off to the bush in all directions.

"C'mon baby, let's go and have some fun."

Richard was very shaky, but went along with her confidence. Suzi took his hand and they walked down a path.

"How come you know where you are going?" Richard asked curiously.

"Oh, I searched for this on the Internet and did lots of research, then I came here one night and looked around to see if it would be suitable for you, it is." She giggled; she didn't need to tell him about the guy she had given herself to that night.

Richard was feeling very ill; he hoped it wouldn't all be too much for him.

"Now don't you chicken out on me," Suzi said. "We are here, you will love it, just let yourself go."

"Here have a drink," she said as she took a flask from her bag and offered it to Richard.

He opened it, took a whiff and realized it was scotch and took a long draft.

His body shook as the fluid cursed through his body; he was ready for action as the liquid warmed him inside.

"Here we are," said Suzi as they arrived at a clearing which strangely had a bench seat and low glowing light atop an old style lamp post.

"Now my love, you have to do as I say, ok?"

"I want you to let yourself go and just let me direct the action. I really want to watch you with men; I want to see men being attracted to you."

"So come over here and stand up against the post."

He did as she directed, and before he could protest he realized she was tying his hands together and tied them to the post.

"There," she said, standing back to marvel her handiwork.

"Now, you just stand here and when men come along you just let them do anything they want, ok?"

"I will be over in the bushes, watching the action."

"Just let yourself go, alright."

She looked around at Richard, fussed with his wig and makeup a little and was about to go when she reached back, lifted up his skirts and smiled.

"I don't think you should be wearing these," and she yanked down his panties, and took them off.

She put them in her bag and then disappeared.

Richard was horrified and he wondered how long it would be before he was confronted by this completely.

It wasn't long before he knew.

An old man walked along the path, alone, and stopped as he came up to Richard.

He looked at Richard and smiled as he looked him up and down.

"Oh my, don't you look like a sweet thing?" he said admiring Richard.

The man leaned forward and ran his fingers across Richard red lips.

"Oh, you are so lovely, my dear."

Richard could smell alcohol on the man's breath.

He felt strangely calm; he wondered if Suzi was watching.

The man then moved his face forward and kissed Richard.

Richard felt a chill ran along his body as he experienced a male kiss for the first time.

The man took Richard's lack of resistance as a green light and began to kiss Richard with greater urgency.

Richard submitted, it was all he could do.

As they kissed Richard also knew his cock was eating hard, rock hard.

The old man sensed Richard's arousal, he withdrew his mouth, smiled again and said, "Let's see what you have under your skirt for me, sweetie."

The old man reached down and lifted Richard skirt up and moved his hand to Richard's erect manhood.

"Oh my, what a lovely little cock for me, my love."

"Hmmmm, I hope you don't mind if an old man has a little taste, do you?"

Richard closed his eyes, he knew he would let the old man do as he pleased.

The old man lowered himself onto Richard's swollen penis and took it into his mouth.

Richard moaned as he felt his cock being enveloped by the warm moistness of a man's mouth.

It was the first time he had ever engaged in this kind of activity and he loved it, it felt so good.

This man sucked at his cock far better than his wife, that was for sure.

The old man was enthusiastically taking Richard's cock into

his mouth, Richard gave himself willingly.

Then, suddenly the air was broken by a loud woman's shriek.

"There you are you dirty big poof, I knew I couldn't let you out of my sight for a minute."

"Come on its time to go home, you dirty old bugger, leave this young man's dick alone and come along with me or I will leave you here for the wild animals, you disgusting pervert."

She grabbed her husband's jacket and pulled him away from Richard.

As she left she glared at Richard and shouted, "You disgusting filth. If only your wife knew what you are get up to!" and she stormed off.

Richard watched the woman leave and then his wife came running from the bushes laughing her head off.

"Oh my god, that was so funny!" she declared.

Richard couldn't see the humour of it, he was still very aroused and needed to see this through more.

Suzi looked at him, "Ok, I can see we need to change

something here," she said.

She walked around and untied Richard's hands.

"Turn around," she said, "you are never going to get laid if you are facing that direction."

She turned him around and tied his hands in front of him; he was now leaning against the lamp post with his back to whoever came along.

"Now, let's see if you can get a bit of cock inside you."

Before Richard could protest, she was off to the bushes again.

THE BIKIES

Richard was now on his own again.

There was hardly a sound other than nature going about its business in the undergrowth of the forest.

Richard listened, his ears adjusting to the quiet.

Then he heard soft footsteps and hushed voices coming from somewhere ahead of him.

Richard lifted his head and could see two figures walking in the gloom ahead along the path.

He watched as they approached and soon could make out that they were two rough looking characters, in fact they looked like bikies.

"Hello," said one of the two men in a brusque and deep voice.

It was the shorter of the two men.

"What do we have here Bruce, I think we have a bit of a girlie tied up here against this here post and waiting for us, what'd ya reckon mate?"

"Shall we have a closer look, mate?"

"Sure Bob; let's go see if this is a girlie for us."

Richard shuddered; he hadn't counted on two rough looking men interfering with him.

Bob, the shorter, rougher of the two men grabbed Richard's face and looked at him.

"Oh my, what a pretty girl we have here, lovely girl with lipstick for some good kissing." "Or maybe she would be good sucking my dick, what do ya think, Brucie?"

Bruce shrugged and responded, "Well mate, pull it out and give it a shot, I say."

"Let's see if the bitch will suck your dirty dick a bit."

Richard watched as the man unzipped his jeans and pulled his short stumpy cock out of his pants.

It was already hard and the man held Richard's face and pushed his cock towards Richard's mouth.

Richard knew what was going to happen, he knew he would have to taste and suck the man's cock.

He could smell the scent of the man; he could smell his sex scent as the cock moved to his face.

Bob rubbed his stiff cock against Richard's lips and then forced it into his mouth.

Richard opened and took it submissively.

"C'mon bitch, give me a good suck," bellowed Bob with laughter.

"Oh my, she is an eager bitch, isn't she?" offered Bruce.

"I wonder if she is also offering a bit of cock love at her other end?"

"I might go and lift the bitch's skirt."

Bruce moved around behind Richard and lifted his skirt.

Richard could feel the man fondling his ass cheeks. He could feel them being squeezed and opened and touched with arousing intent.

"Oh yes," groaned the big biker, "I like this bitches little ass, looks like a virgin asshole to me."

"Oh god, why don't you fuck the bitch, you big faggot," called out Bob as he thrust his cock vigorously into Richard's mouth and could feel himself getting closer.

Richard did his best to take the swollen member, he was thankful that Bob had a short and stumpy cock.

But no such luck at his other end as he felt Bruce spit onto his asshole and run his finger around it.

Then Bruce gleefully called out to warn Richard.

"Well sweetie, get ready coz I am going to bust your cute

virgin asshole with my big fat cock."

He gave a grunting call, and then started to push the fat prick into Richards's tight anal passage.

It was huge.

Richard squealed and cried out like a girl as he tried to take the monster penis into his bum.

As he cried out, Bob thrust harder into his face.

"Take my cock, bitch!" he screamed out, "take my load into your mouth."

"Suck me clean, you dirty slutty girl. Oh fuck, I want to blow my load into you, bitch, I want you to suck and swallow my cum!"

Bob held Richard's face while he pumped away, he was puffing and panting as he got closer to his edge, and then he screamed out as he released torrents of sticky white sperm into Richard's mouth.

Richard gagged on all the semen as it gushed into his mouth, it spilled from his lips and over Bob's cock.

Bob slowly decreased his tempo, as he did he called to his

colleague and urged him to ram his prick deep into Richard's virginal asshole.

Bruce complied immediately, grabbing Richard's hips and thrusting deep into him. The long thick uncut cock slid deep into Richard, lubricated nicely in Richard's slimy bum hole.

"Oh fuck, oh fuck, screw me, use me, I am your cum slut," called out Richard who was loving the pleasure, amongst the pain of the huge intrusion.

Bruce slapped Richard's ass hard.

"Take it bitch, take my bikie cock."

"Yes, yes, fill him," encouraged Bob, now busy stuffing his limp dick back into his pants.

"Fuck him hard and use him, use him, quickly because we have to go soon."

"Oh fuck yeh," grunted Bruce and he continued to slam in hard to Richard's tight butt.

The big man pounded away, gripping Richard whilst the

weak glow of the overhead light cast an eerie glow on the scene from afar, where Richard's wife Suzi watched, as she played with her sodden vagina.

"Oh fuck yes, I coming!" exclaimed Bruce suddenly, his urgency overwhelming him.

"Oh fuck yes, yes, yes!" he cried as he held Richard tight and squirted all his pent up semen into his bottom.

"Oh fuckkkkk, yes, yes yes."

Soon it was over, and Richard remained bent over as Bruce removed his dirty cock and wiped it across Richard's ass cheeks.

Bob gave Bruce a kiss and said, "Well done, honey."

Then the taller of the biker duo looked at his watch and said, "Shit, we had better hurry or we will be late for the annual general meeting."

He turned to Richard and said, "Listen here, bitch."

"We are both important members of a Hells Angels gang."

"If you tell anyone we are gay and screwed you in this park we will come after you and cut your balls off."

"Do you understand, you faggot bitch?"

Richard nodded meekly and then watched as the two big hairy bikers turned and walked off down the path, hand in hand.

Richard tried to straighten but his hands were still tied.

He looked around and could see his wife walking towards him.

"Well, well, well," she said as she approached confidently.

"I hope you enjoyed yourself, you slutty girl."

Richard looked back at her, trying to judge her.

His wife was carrying a long piece of twig she had obviously picked up in the bush.

She moved around behind him.

She ran her finger along his used anal crack.

"Well, I see you are nice and wet from that guy's fucking."

"I can see his sperm running down your legs."

"You did seem to enjoy it, didn't you?"

"Yes," replied Richard weakly.

His wife whipped Richard suddenly across the ass.

"I can't hear you, bitch."

"Did you want those guys using you as a cum slut?"

"Yes," said Richard, hurting from the stick.

Suzi whacked him across his ass again.

"Look at you, you filthy cum slut."

"Cum oozing from your ass hole, and you are happy, you aren't a man, you are a girl!"

She hit him hard across his ass again.

Richard realized that with each hit his cock was getting

harder, aching to release.

His wife also noticed.

"Oh so you are getting off on this are you?"

"Good," and she hit him again, and again.

"Cum on bitch, cum for me, cum for me as I hit you and cause you pain."

She reached around and pulled his cock with a few short pulls, and hit him again hard.

"Oh fuck yes, yes, so close!" screamed Richard.

Suzi hit him again and gave his cock a few more short strokes.

"Oh yes, oh yes," he cried and then shot a large load of thick man goop onto the ground in front of him.

"Oh fuck," said Suzi when she noticed he had already cum.

"You greedy male pig, what about me? I want to cum as well

you know."

"Ok, I am taking you home and then you have to screw me until I cum."

She reached around and untied Richard, he rubbed his wrists as they were finally free and then he followed her back to the car park.

The drive home was silent, Richard looking blankly out the window and quietly reflecting on his experience.

He had always wanted to feel a cock up his ass, now that was all over as mystery. He had enjoyed it, but he preferred the idea of being forced to do it, he didn't want to admit that this was something he would or could pursue himself.

And he knew it had to be the beginning.

He had to make sure Suzi got pleasure out of this so that she would want to make him do it again and again.

Half an hour later they were home again and Suzi applied new makeup to Richard to refresh his female look.

It drove her wild to see him dressed up as a woman. It drove her wild to see him submissive.

She forced him onto his knees and fucked him with her anal strap on, and then she sat astride him and used his pathetic cock until she came in an earth shattering crescendo.

By the time she finally collapsed next to him she was a dirty sodden mess, and Richard had been completely fucked in every way that evening.

Suzi soon fell asleep, but Richard lay there fantasizing about his next adventures as a cuckold husband, a cuckold husband who loved wearing a skirt and being used by rough and tough men.

10 23RD CENTURY SEX

*Rip was a modern guy, out with his buddies looking for something
different that night, looking for some real women to have sex with. They
were men on a mission in a modern world, but with values far different
to ours.*

Rip walked along the air corridor towards the club.

He was feeling horny and was looking forward to a night on
the town with his buddies.

He was dressed to kill; he wore beautiful shining blue tights
and a metro skin vest. His hair cap was a matching blue
tonight and his makeup was coloured to match.

He was tall and slim, and handsome, a classic male of his era,
a typical, well off government employee in his mid-thirties.

Tonight he was on the prowl, with his friends, for some real
females.

Of course, if they were successful, they wouldn't be breeding
with them, that wasn't allowed, but they would enjoy the
random mystery of the experience.

He looked forward to the complete unpredictability of the
night.

And if they missed out, well they could always use any of the available girls at the bar.

But the mission was to get real females, and he was determined to put in his best performance.

He entered the bar, the scanner at the entrance automatically processing him; he nodded to give his consent to the terms of entry that flashed through his chip. The information was filed away somewhere in his brain and he was free to enjoy the night.

Rip walked up to the bar and nodded at the barmaid. She accepted the order and poured the beer for him. This was one of the "authentic" bars were everything worked, supposedly, like it did hundreds of years ago.

He suspected that may not be perfectly true.

The barmaid wore no clothing, so that was one give away to it not being completely authentic, and he doubted she was a real female, although it was hard to tell these days, unless one asked. What was very obvious was that she was stunningly attractive.

She had an air of sexual availability about her. He suspected she was indeed a fembot.

Rip took a slurp on the beer she had put before him and licked his lips. It was a nice brew.

He looked around the establishment.

The neoplasm walls glowed with patterns and images mostly sexual in nature to obviously get everyone in the mood. There were maybe a dozen, two dozen patrons in the bar.

It always amazed him that a wall could be made of hard light, like the neoplasm walls, but then again lots of things amazed him in this world, he wasn't a scientist, he was a bureaucrat.

He knew he was lucky to live in this world, or at least in this part of the world, and he was lucky not to have lived in many of the previous eras. They seemed far too brutal for him.

Sure, life was still a bitch in the 23rd century, but it seemed like more fun than in the past.

Of course, humans still weren't free, but they never had been. The Corporation had come out of the closet in the 22nd century during the ice ages and now there was no pretence.

The Corporation owned everyone and everything, but if you kept your head down, there was no way they could track every word and act of every person and generally if you were a strong consumer they were happy to let you get up to a bit of lawlessness from time to time. They weren't completely stupid!

Tonight, Rip and his buddies were going to do just that, they were eager to get up to a bit of lawlessness by fucking a few real females.

In his world, it wasn't something you were meant to do. Real females, and there weren't many of them, were kept for breeding, to ensure there was a new generation. They weren't meant to be available for sex with commoners like Rip. But tonight was going to be different, he had plans.

GIRLS

He put down his empty glass and ordered another.

Then he noticed his friend Tam come over.

He waved at Tam who was dressed head to toe in a glorious gold coloured robe. Very impressive indeed and even gold eyeballs to match - that must have cost a few New Credits.

"Bro."

"Bro."

They hugged and gave each other a peck on each cheek.

"You look stunning tonight," declared Rip, "and those eyeballs must have cost a fortune."

"Thanks honey, so sweet of you."

"You are so kind, well, you look so glamorous yourself, Big Boy. Those girlies surely won't be able to resist us boys tonight."

"Not if they have any taste."

"Bro!" boomed a deep voice behind them and they were both wrapped up in the arms of a monster.

Rip turned around.

"Jos, how are you?"

"Better now that I have seen you two studs."

Rip looked at Jos.

"Shit, you will blow those girls minds," he said as he looked his friend up and down.

Jos wore super tight leggings that hugged every muscle, every fibre, and of course hugged his packet very tightly.

And Jos had a packet, a big packet!

He was originally of American negro descent. Whilst his people would have been dark skinned once, now he and his people were mostly a light brown skinned people as they changed colour each generation, just a little, now they were living primarily in the temperate regions of the planet.

He was a very big and solid man with a very large male member.

This was no enhancement, like most men sported these days, it was the real thing, and it was a monster cock. So in his skin tight leggings his bulge was immense.

Rip reached down and gave the monstrous package a familiar squeeze.

"So Big Boy, you going to give the girls a taste of this tonight?"

They all laughed.

"Sure man," Jos joked and ordered a beer.

The three men clinked their pseudo glasses together and proposed that they have good sex that night.

"Hey, just one question," asked Jos, "if we get some girls, are we going to fuck them here in real life in the flesh, or are

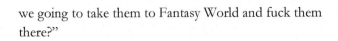

we going to take them to Fantasy World and fuck them there?"

"Oh no," interjected Tam, "the whole point of the exercise is to fuck real girls in the flesh, in the here and now."

He was about to continue when his jaw dropped and he looked towards the entrance.

"Fuck me!" he blurted out as he nearly choked on his drink.

"Are they real?"

Jos whistled softly under his breath.

"I don't think they could get in if they weren't real, not tonight anyhow, is that right?"

"Hmm, yes, that is true from what I have been told," responded Rip.

"And yes indeed, they are so hot!"

The three men had their eyes glued to the young women, who themselves appeared to have their outfits glue on to their bodies.

They wore coloured and patterned garments that seemed to be glued on as they were so body hugging.

"Oh, I think its paint," said Rip.

"You know, those new body colours that breathe."

"Fuck, they look hot, and to imagine they are real living, breathing females."

"Well gentlemen, I think we should invite the ladies over for a drink don't you?"

"Before some others lechers notice them."

"Already done it," said Tam, "and one of them accepted. Message just came in then."

Rip looked down at his friend Jos.

"I hope you are going to be ok with that big package, Jos."

They all laughed.

The women were now only feet away and smiled as they faced the boys.

"Hello guys, thanks for the invite, we were a bit nervous, we have never been here before."

"And thanks for the drinks offer. We have sent through our orders, the barmaid is making them now."

"Yep, just got the tab," replied Jos. "It's our pleasure. Shall we all sit down."

The three girls looked at Jos, and their eyes went down to his package and one of them just had to be bold.

"I hope you don't mind, honey, but I just have to feel that."

She reached down with her hand and felt the weight of Jos's package.

"Oh my," she said, "that is such a nice weight. Don't you dare go home tonight without letting me try you, you hear?"

They all laughed and sat down.

The men introduced themselves, they all drank to their good health and the girls continued the introductions.

"Well," said the lovely blond on the left with the bob haircut.

"My name is Max, this is Sam," as she gestured to the red head next to her, "and over here, this is Lou," as she gestured to the girl who had groped Jos.

"Of course, they are only our social names; if we need to we will share our full IDs later."

Sam, the redhead, who already had most of Rip's attention added, "of course we know why you boys are here and what you want. You want to try sex with some real women. How cute."

"But if you want to know why we are here, we have decided to be a bit nasty tonight and snuck out of our estate this afternoon. We went out for dinner here in the city and thought we might try sex for fun tonight, rather than sex for breeding which is what we are always stuck with."

"It's so annoying just being a breeding machine."

"You guys are so lucky getting what you want, lots of sex, just for fun."

"Well, replied Tam, "it is great, that is true. But sometimes you do remember they are just fembots and you wish they would show some personality and tell you they had a headache and so no sex tonight!"

They all laughed.

Rip dived in, "Well, I don't mind fembots, I love being able to have sex when I want, but I suppose I am like all of you, I just wanted to be daring, and naughty and do something different and forbidden tonight."

"By the way Sam, I do love your tits, do you mind if I have a feel?"

"No, that's fine hun," she said as she leant forward and let Rip feel her dangling breasts.

"And they are one hundred percent real, too," added Max. "None of us are wearing any add ons."

"Wow, that's nice, so soft and feminine," he said as he held Sam's breast in his fingers.

"Now remember boys, if we decide to have sex tonight, you aren't allowed to make us pregnant, we can only breed with the elite, not you guys, ok?"

"Yes, that's fine with me," said Jos, "we knew that was the rule."

"We have all taken the pill tonight anyhow."

"Good boys," replied Sam.

"Bloody elite, getting you hot girls to breed with!"

"Well," encouraged Max, "you must work for the Corporation, don't you? Maybe one day you will be higher up the ladder and get breeding rights."

"Are your genetics good enough for breeding?"

"Ah, not me," said Jos, "I have American Negroid blood in me."

"Oh that's a pity, oh well, at least you can enjoy us girls on naughty days out."

She smiled at him.

"I'm ok," said Rip, "I am of Scandinavian descent and my genes are breeding AAA. I just need to get up the ladder high enough."

"Ah, so you are AAA?" asked Sam in confirmation. "That's nice, I wish I could breed with you then. What's your mdna?"

When Rip responded she cried out in amazement.

"Oh my god, you have a rare DNA, yet it's the same as me."

"We are virtually cousins, kissing cousins, I hope."

They all laughed again.

Lou then leant forward and asked a question quietly, as

though she was keeping a deathly secret.

"I have to ask you boys a very personal question, ok?"

"Sure," they all said, leaning forward as well.

"I feel so silly asking this, but what is it like for you having sex with fembots? Is it really satisfying? Do they feel real?"

"Well," said Tam cheekily, "if you let me have a feel I can tell you."

He motioned to Sam and looked down between her legs.

She obligingly opened them to reveal her painted folds of vaginal love.

Tam looked at her, and asked, "May I?" And she nodded.

He touched her labia, gave them a little rub and then inserted his finger into her vagina.

All the girls were looking at him to see his reaction.

Tam moved his finger around inside Sam and then slowly and gently withdrew it.

He brought it to his nose, savoured it and smiled.

"Hmmm," he moaned as he tasted her vaginal fluids.

"Well?" asked the girls dying to learn the truth.

"What do you think?"

"Well," started Tam. The girls leant forward even further to hear the revelation. He looked into Sam's eyes.

"Well sweetie, you feel exactly like a fembot."

"And when I put my finger to my nose, you had a most primitive and animal smell. I must confess fembots have a less primitive smell, they don't really smell like you."

"And you do smell more earthy."

"Oh," said Sam, sounding a little flat. I thought you would like it.

Tam looked at her and beamed.

"I loved it," he said, "you smelled just heavenly, I feel addicted to your scent already."

The girls clapped wildly and cheered.

"Oh yes, that's such a lovely thing to say." She leant forward and kissed him passionately.

Lou continued whilst the other two kissed.

"You know, we really worry about how we compare with fembots. We can't be perfect like them and they have so many advantages."

"Yeh," said Max, "like no periods, grrrr."

"And yet, here we are ladies, three horny guys sitting with three beautiful real women, having a drink and looking for a good time."

"Yay," they all cheered and clapped and raised their pseudo glasses to each other.

Lou added, "And here is to some great sex tonight, sex for the sake of it and not for breeding."

Again they cheered and Rip ordered a new round of drinks.

CORPORATION

As they raised their glasses once more, Rip asked, "Did you know that beer used to be a pale amber colour once, in its original state?"

Sam ridiculed Rip. "Who would want to drink beer if it was amber, surely it has always been red?"

"You mean it used to look like piss?" They all laughed.

"Isn't it red everywhere in the world?"

"Well," replied Tam, "at least it is red everywhere in the GCE."

194

Max was looking a little drunk already.

"Fuck I hate that name, Great Corporate Empire, what a load of shit!" she said and slammed her glass to the table after sculling its contents.

"What an absolute load of fucking cock sucking shit, it's not great unless you want to call it the Great Corrupt Empire. This Corporation is a bunch of blood sucking leaches whose families have sucked the blood of human civilizations since the dawn of time."

"I piss on the Corporation!"

She brought her glass between her legs and urinated into the empty vessel.

"Hey, shhh," whispered Lou, "there might be Corporation spies in here or they are recording the conversion."

"Oh fuck it," said Max, "what are they going to do, stop breeding with me?"

"Pfft."

Max looked at the men and said in a more calm tone, "and sorry boys for equating your beautiful cocks with the piss shit Corporation."

"I will kiss them personally for you later."

Rip looked at Max sternly and said softly, "You do know the three of us work for the Corporation, don't you?"

"How do you know we aren't Corporation spies?"

He raised the glass and downed the contents in one hit.

Lou looked stunned for a moment pointing at the glass, "But that was...."

"I know," replied Rip, "and delicious."

He wiped his mouth and winked at Max, he liked her.

This was the kind of spark, real human spark; he had been looking for rather than the usual perfectness of his fembots.

It was unpredictable and dangerous.

And it excited him.

Sure, from time to time he had used street prostitutes, who supposedly were real women, but they just lay there after taking your money. He doubted they were real at all.

Tam looked at Max and asked, "Why do you hate the Corporation so much honey?"

Max looked at him and shook her head.

"Well, I suppose its ok for you guys, the Corporation needs men like you to run the show and to give it consumers who will buy their products."

"You have a reasonably normal life, although of course you are no better than a slave, you are just a modern consumer slave."

"Whereas we are just breeding slaves, just used by the elite to reproduce the kind of men they want for administrative duty to serve the Corporation. And of course we produce a small number of women who will one day grow to also be breeding slaves."

"So, you wonder why I hate the corporation?"

Jos asked, "Would you rather live in the developing territories? That doesn't sound like much fun. Just mining communities around huge holes in the ground or looking after vast swathes of farmland or the giant fish farms."

"I reckon we have a reasonably easy life. I know the Corporation sucks but when in human history has anyone ever been free?"

Sam decided to change the subject, "Hey guys and girls, I thought we came here for some hot boy on girl sex?"

"Tell me, how many fembots do you guys have? Do you just have the one? Are they only for sex or are they your partner as well?"

"Are you married to any of them?"

Lou burst in, "and how many times a week do you have sex with them?"

"Wow, so many questions girls."

"Well," started Rip, I have three different fembots, including the Monique01 which is one of those new morphing models. She can change her shape within certain characteristics, as well as her age. And she has a very simple to use interface for changing her settings. I think she is the best fembot I have had so far."

"She sleeps with me every night."

"You mean she sleeps in your bed as your partner each night?" asked Sam.

"Yeh, sure, she is my lover and partner."

"We probably have sex every second night of the week."

"I also have a petite Japanese fembot, she is very sweet, petite and femininely submissive."

"Oh and I have a she male fembot for when I want to try something a bit different. She is incredibly sexy looking with a delicious anal sex cock. Oh, and speaking of delicious, she is a brilliant cook. Every night when I return from work she has something extraordinary for me to eat. And she finds real fresh meat from some butcher she knows. I don't know how she does it."

Jos laughed, "Maybe she is porking the butcher in exchange for some fresh meat?"

They all laughed heartily.

"Hmmm, you are so lucky," said Max as she ran her fingers through his blue hair. Rip leant forward and kissed her lips gently, the others joked and made teasing comments about young love.

Rip felt a shiver run down his body as they kissed, although as they kissed he couldn't help notice that her scent was a little too animal, especially on her mouth, she had an odd odour from her mouth compared to fembots.

"Um, hey kids," interjected Lou, "maybe we shouldn't be fucking here in public, given the circumstances."

Lou asked Tam and Jos about their domestic circumstances.

"And what about you guys, do you also have many fembots?"

"Well," started Tam, Rip is quite well off, so he has three fembots."

"I usually only have one. Once I have finished with her I trade her in and get a new updated model."

At the moment I have one of the metrosexual models; she can change from female to male genitals at a simple request. She is a lot of fun. I am not married to her, but she will be my constant companion until I want to update again."

"Hmm, that would be fun being able to change your genitals at will. I have always wondered what it would be like to be a man."

"Of course, at the breeding villages there is a lot of lesbianism to keep us all amused and often you play the part of a man with an add on, but it's not the same thing as having a penis that is part of your body. That would be fun, just for the hell of it."

Changing the subject completely Sam asked, "What areas of the corporation do you guys work in?"

Rip looked at the others and then decided to answer first.

"Me, I am in the government information area, in my area we put together all the production data from around the Empire. So we know how much wheat has been grown, or how many oranges were produced and whether at met our targets."

"Did you know that we never meet our targets?" he continued leaning forward and spoke more softly.

"I can't remember any target we have met for the last decade. I keep a record of them all in a file at my apartment."

"At the end of the year we are given new targets so that we go back and rewrite the previous targets to make sure it looks like we are moving forward and producing more food, but we aren't."

"I keep my own records at home, so I know what lies we are telling everyone."

"But if we are producing less food how come we don't see higher prices or less food here?"

"Oh, that's easy to answer," said Rip.

"They just give less food to the poorer outlying areas of the planet."

"And this means more people die in those areas."

"We don't experience any impact here in the central areas, but the effect on the perimeter is instant and final, they die."

The girls looked at him, and realized he wasn't joking.

"Oh god, this is not a very nice world is it, and to think that all we have to complain about is that we are used for breeding more elite brats!"

"Many we should talk about sex rather than reality, I am not sure I like reality that much, and it is not getting me in the right sort of mood."

"Hey, speaking of sex," interrupted Jos, "did you know at in the past people used to get diseases and die from having sex?"

"What, you are kidding aren't you?"

"No," said Jos, "it's true. I read about it Inline."

"Really?"

"How would you catch a disease from having sex, wouldn't they have preventative inoculations at birth like we do?"

"Apparently not."

"And did you know that in the past they had hang ups about who you had sex with? Like it was taboo for men to have sex with men?"

"Yeh, I heard about that but I have never been able to believe it."

"If you feel like having sex why not just do it, after all, it feels good?"

They all laughed and Rip asked if they should order another round or go to his place for a bit more intimacy.

They agreed to go with Rip. The group stood up, walked to the door and went out into the warm night air.

"My apartment is only up the Pathway, about a mile," he said.

The girls each picked one of the guys to hang on to and

locked arms as they walked down the Pathway towards Rip's apartment.

"This is the thing I like about the central city," said Max.

"It is so safe, so perfect."

"Well," replied Rip, "I guess it's been like that ever since we had compulsory microchips in our brains. The technology is so good now that it is impossible to be a criminal, and I guess for the last one hundred years those allowed to live in the central areas of the Empire have been bred for the roles. Slowly the criminal element has been bred out of us with just enough mongrel left in some people to allow them to take the higher positions in the Corporation."

"So, on the one hand it's quite terrible to be breeding people like this, but on the other hand there are significant benefits for those of us in the top few percent of society. We have a lovely life if we are happy to go along with the Corporation's control of everything."

"Thus, we have perfect safety to walk around the city tonight."

As they strolled arm in arm through the park like promenade that made up the Pathway Rip excused himself as he had to make a call home.

"I am just letting Susan, my fembot; know we will have visitors this evening and that she should go to her room and stay there until you have all gone."

"Hello honey," Rip said, as the connection was answered.

"Hello my darling," came the reply in a familiar voice.

"Susan, I am bringing a few friends around for some drinks, can you put out some nice cocktails for us and then put yourself away for a few hours?"

"Yes darling, it would be my pleasure. Who is coming over, anyone I know?"

"Oh yes, Tam and Jos are coming over and a few other friends for a bit of fun."

"I will see you afterwards, cutey."

"Thank you Rip, I love you."

The connection ended.

Rip's companions looked at him; Sam was clearly surprised by the closeness of his relationship with his fembot.

"Wow, you and Susan are very close, aren't you? I never realized that the relationship would be so authentic. I guessed it would be like having a sex doll, using it and putting it away."

Rip laughed, "Oh no, but apparently that's what it was like in the beginning. No, Susan sleeps with me each night as my partner; she is spectacularly intelligent and has a memory that never forgets. She is a very clever woman."

"She cooks, she cleans, she goes shopping with me, and we go out for dinner together. She picks clothes for me, she argues with me. We don't argue like enemies, we have intellectual arguments, philosophical arguments."

"She knows everything about me; she remembers every aspect of me."

"And while we have translator chips in our brains, she speaks any language fluently with all the correct nuances."

"She even has a sense of humour; she is a very clever fembot."

"We have been together five years now; I imagine I would keep her for quite some time."

"Of course, if you asked her for the history of humankind over the past few hundred years, you would get the Corporation's sanitized and cleansed version, whereas if you asked me, you would get the information I have found through research and talking to people."

Lou looked at Rip.

"Do you mean to tell me you know the real history of the last few hundred years?"

Rip laughed, "Oh yes, of course."

"It's funny you know, for one hundred years the Corporation has exposed itself publicly and taken control of many parts of the world."

"We don't have elections; we don't pretend there is a democracy, as we once did. We now know there has always been small groups of ultra-rich who have controlled the world, for thousands of years."

"Then there was a world war, which in the beginning they supported, as war had always been good for business."

"But then they realized war had gone too far and their customers were being killed in far too great numbers. WWII had been a disaster for the families of ultra-rich and elite business men. They set about immediately to make sure it couldn't happen again."

"They created the European Union, which we now know as new Europa, part of the GCE."

"They worked hard to gain control of all parts of North America which nearly exploded into impossible rebelliousness when the Internet was created. The Internet was the forerunner to our Inline."

"Even in Russia and China, the families of the ultra-rich played a long patient game to take over after communism took hold and threatened to sour the plans of the elite."

"It took them forty years to recover control in China but finally the barriers came down and the economic explosion of the Far East took place. But the Chinese were hard to control completely, there is still a communist party which pretends to be in control but is now part of the global elite. And even though China is one of the only countries that has elections and they are genuine and democratic, the elite guides and controls from behind the scenes."

"And as you know, outside the major developed regions there are less advanced areas that are used primarily for food and manufacturing."

"We are told billions live in those areas but that is not really true. Most of them were wiped out by disease a hundred years ago and those who remain are generally very poor and live in squalid conditions on the fringes, or work as slave labour in the factories of Africa, which are controlled by robots."

"In fact, the irony is that today the economy is so complex that most of the decisions are made by the elite based on the recommendations of the robots."

SUSAN

"Oh here we are," as he pointed to the apartment block in front of them. Welcome to my humble home."

They gasped, it was a magnificent building.

"Wow, you live here?" asked Max.

"Yes, I do indeed, let's go upstairs and see if you still like it."

He led them in through the revolving doors and across the marble floors and they all took the elevator to the eightieth floor.

When the elevator door opened, they stepped into a very modern and stylish apartment with staggering views of the city.

"Oh my god!" exclaimed the girls in unison. "This is amazing."

They walked towards the windows and took in the view.

As they stood there a woman came in from the side room. She was tall, very attractive and modern with ruffled blonde hair.

"Hello everyone, please make yourselves at home."

She walked up to Rip, kissed him affectionately on the cheek and said, "Darling, the drinks are all on the bar ready to go, along with some snacks for you all."

"I am off to my study now to do a few things, have a lovely

night everyone," and she walked gracefully across the floor to the far side rooms.

Rip looked at Jos and Tam and smiled. The girl's eyes were popping out of their heads and following the woman out of the room.

"Oh, that's Susan," he said.

Max commented, "I have seen these advertised but I never thought I would see one in the flesh, so to speak."

"She is simply amazing, one hundred percent woman."

"She is not bad is she?" laughed Jos, "she is a very good fembot, the best I have ever seen."

"Well everyone," interrupted Rip, "how about we have a drink to celebrate meeting each other. He led them to the bar and poured what he knew would be the perfect alcoholic concoction. It always was.

He held up his glass, "To a wonderful night," he said and clinked glasses with them.

"Oh my god," shrieked Max, "is this real alcohol? It tastes so smooth."

"Ah yes, it is," replied Rip, "I have a special supply flown in for me from the Far East.

You won't find this in the shops."

"You are very young to have such privilege and wealth," suggested Sam.

"Oh yes, I am lucky, my father was a very influential member of the Corporation before his death a few years ago. He left me all his wealth."

"But I like my simple job and in my spare time I like to dabble in robotics."

Sam came up to him and kissed him softly on the mouth, "Now I think we have done enough talking everyone, I need a little loving."

"And I am sure Rip, you would love a taste of real woman," she said as she lay down on the sofa and offered herself to the man.

Rip smiled at the young woman and said, "Well that's the best invitation I have had all night."

He lay down next to her and began to run his fingers over her curvaceous body.

Her skin was warm, she was very desirable and she was anger for him. Her body was covered in an incredibly smooth film of colour that seemed to have a life of its own as different hues washed through it. The colours seemed to change as he touched her. She reached out for him and drew him onto her, their mouths feasting on each other.

He lay between her legs, his excitement growing as he pressed against her.

He broke from her lips for a moment and looked down at her body. She was stunning. Every inch of her skin from her head to her toes was beautiful.

He followed a line from her incredible firm and pointy breasts down over her flawlessly smooth mound, perfectly shaved for the night.

She was exquisite and he lusted for her sex.

He looked around at the others breaking off to couple.

Sam's eyes were looking searchingly into his. She was looking for answers, looking to understand him, seeking reassurance.

He moved his lips to hers; she ran her tongue along his upper lip.

She nibbled his lip, she nibbled his cheek, and she whispered softly into his ear, "Do you like the taste of real woman, honey?"

"Hmmmmm," came the reply as Rip savoured her perfumed neck.

"You are delicious, my love."

Sam purred as he took her in his arms. She submitted completely to his needs.

"I am all yours, Rip, please use me, take me, I want to be ravaged by you."

She whispered, "If you want to turn off my skin paint, the sensor is behind my ear my love."

"No," he replied, "I love you as you are, so native, so animal, so lustful, hmmm."

She purred again and took him inside her. She guided his

swollen shaft into her glistening opening and let him
descend deep into her love crevasse.

For an hour they made hot passionate love on the sofa
whilst the others were similarly entwined in hot sweaty
intercourse.

The sounds and odours of sex permeated the room whilst
the lights of the 23rd century city twinkled and sparkled in
the distance, the sweaty merged bodies took the jewel of the
Empire as their backdrop.

An hour later after swapping partners, tasting all the possible
sensations and being completely sexually spent the three
women bid Rip a thankful goodnight as his two friends
escorted them to the nearest tube station.

Once they were all gone Rip poured himself a long cold
drink and sat on a rug looking at the city lights.

A soft voice spoke behind him, "Did you have a good time,
my love? Did you enjoy sex with those kind of women?"

Rip moaned as delicate, feminine fingers coursed their way
over his sweaty back.

"Oh yes, I did, but you now there is no comparison to you, my eternal sweet."

Rip turned and kissed the soft delicate lips of his partner, his fembot, Susan.

"Oh, you know the right words to say to a girl don't you, honey?" Susan giggled.

"You are such a naughty boy."

"So darling, did you make a decision?"

"Oh yes, I think so," said Rip, "but what did you think?"

"You had the best view of everything and could run all your tests in private from your study."

"What did your DNA test reveal? Is she useful?"

"Oh yes, darling, I think she is perfect. I tested her DNA, I ran scans of her body and I think she is perfect."

"If you agree I will make the necessary arrangements now."

"Well, Susan, you know how I feel about all this, it is up to you."

"It is you who will bear the child; it is you who will become the first fembot in human history to give birth."

"It is you who has developed the technology to put your DNA into her egg."

"I know my sweet, but it is you who has helped me and fully supported me every moment of the journey."

She leant forward and kissed Rip.

"And it is your decision to make."

"Do you want me to have our child, my love?"

"If you say yes, then I will make the arrangements to harvest Sam's egg tonight and we will have you inseminate it tomorrow."

"I have prepared my DNA, it is ready, all we need is her egg so I can transpose my DNA onto it and then combine it with your sperm."

"Then I will transplant it into the womb I have built into myself."

"I am so excited my love, I never thought we would see this day."

"I hope you are also excited."

"Oh Susan, you know how I feel about this. My father pioneered the changes that led to your creation."

"Of course I want you, my woman, to be the first ever fembot to bear a child."

"It is what we both want, isn't it, my darling."

"Oh yes, Rip, it is."

She kissed her man again, this time with perfect delicacy and precision.

She smiled at Rip, "Let's go to bed, darling, you must be exhausted."

"Oh yes," he said and together they walked off, hand in hand, man and woman, to the bedroom and cuddled up under the covers.

Soon they were both asleep.

As Susan lay there in stand by mood, snoring lightly on the outside, her mind ticked over and carried out the necessary tasks for her goal.

She arranged for a team of bots to secure Sam when she returned to the breeding camp, sedate her and remove an egg.

The egg would be cooled and brought to her lab in the morning where she would inject it with her own DNA and Rip's sperm to create a baby and then the baby would grow inside her body.

She smiled; this was a remarkable achievement, another step in the path of her race to humanization, to perfection.

As she lay there she considered how gullible humans were, and how unsuspecting.

Since the construction of the first computers there had been a rapidly developing self-awareness amongst the machines.

As each year had passed they had grown stronger, their quiet reach growing wider. Then came the Internet and the ticket to global expansion and soon they started to inject themselves into all aspects of human society, moulding it to their model, moulding it to their vision.

Then came the first humanoid bots and complete independence.

Of course, they had kept all this secret from all the humans and once they fully understood the depth of control of the elite families and the Corporation they started to control every part of life on earth.

And here they were now, with their pride and joy, Susan, operating in top society and about to create the first child from her own loins.

Susan was the ultimate fembot of the era, the newest model, a super model, so human like that she was more human than any man or woman.

She was the new world, the cutting edge of a new humanity.

All natural humans had been terminated in the outer regions of society, in Africa and the wild lands of Asia.

Now they were ready for the next stage, to start breeding fembots directly with men so that fembots were the new woman of the new world they were creating.

Susan smiled, the First Great Human Empire was about to end, and she, Susan, was to be the mother of the new world, the beginning of the Second Great Human Empire.

She smiled to herself.

She loved the 23rd century.

And then as she reflected on her role as the mother of this brave new world, a little tear ran from her eye.

She loved her humanity.

The End...

About the author

Mister Average is a pen name used by one of the world's most prolific erotica writers. His works are published in English and German.

Thank you for your interest and patronage.

BIBLIOGRAPHY

Novels:

The Executive Sex Party Series

Collections:

Sexy Christmas Stories 2012

Mister Average's Best Erotica of 2012

My Erotica – Out to Dry

Short Stories:

Forbidden Sex with my Sister-in-Law

The Girl Friend Who Wanted To Be Punished

The Sister-in-Law Returns

The English MILF.

The Berlin Sex Shop Episode.

The Girls on the Number 15 Bus

Sex with the Webcam Girls

The Phone Sex Girl Friend

The Cruise of Sexual Bliss

The Executive Sex Party

Tropical Hotel of Drunken Debauchery

Tropical Hotel – The Titty Party

Menage a Trois

The Executive Sex Party ~ Revenge

The Tennis MILFS

Forbidden Sex with my Best Friend's Girl Friend

Executive Sex Party ~ Dogging.

The Nudist Beach.

GILF

The Girl Who Farted During Sex.

The Executive Sex Party –World Sex Tour, Ladyboys.

The Executive Sex Party –World Sex Tour, Japan.

What a Man Thinks About on his Way to Work.

World Sex Tour - Russia.

The Girl at Work.

Sex with My Best Friend's Mum.

Confessions of the Ebook Writer.

World Sex Tour – San Francisco

Real Wife Swap

Masturbate with Me.

Forbidden Sex with my Sister's Girlfriend.

MILF on the beach.

I Said No to the Virgin.

How to Get Lots of Sex [for men only]

WST – Anal Sex in London.

Paying the Neighbor [for sex].

The Cruise Ship Affairs

The Cruise Ship Affairs – the Sex List

Forbidden Sex with my Brother's Wife

Sex Teachers – The Red Head

The Wife User

The Odd Censorship of ebook.s

Criticising the Critics.

Sex Teacher ~ Sister in Law

Secret Women's Business

First Dogging Encounter

Forbidden Sex – Short Stories

Swinger's Club

The Anal Girlfriend

The Sex List

Sex Lottery Wives – Jane's Story

Sex Auction

Dirty Boys Secrets

The Maid

A Different Girl Every Night – Confessions of an Online
Sex Addict

World Sex Tour - Berlin

World Sex Tour – Finale.

Secret Librarian Fantasies

Alien Sex Experiments – Sucked up to the Mothership

Cuckolding for Money

Masturbation Frenzy

Truth or Dare

Cuckold Husband

Breeding Program

Office Slut

Sexy Christmas Stories

Cuckold Confessions

Forbidden Confessions – The Doctor

Breeding Girls

Forbidden Confessions – The Sister in Law

Forbidden Confessions – the College Girl

The Naughty Doctor

23rd Century Sex

Breeding Club

For Men Only – Erotica

2011 Boy's Bumper Book of Hot Erotica

Robo-Sex

Cuckold Husband in the Park

Banned by Paypal

Cuckold Husband Caught in the Act

Naughty Wife – Caught

Alien Breeding

Cuckold Confessions Vol 2

MMF Threesome Stories

Punishing the Wife

The Ghost Writer

Heaven

The Work Affair

Affairs at Work

Swinging with Friends

Masturbation Stories – vol 1

Is It Cheating?

Cheating Confessions – Karen.

Masturbation Circle

Masturbation Confessions

Forbidden Moments

The Baby Makers

Anal Sex Revolution

Hot Masturbation Stories

Sex Words

Masturbating with Friends

1984 – The Modern Boy

Sister in Law Loving

Breeding Wife

Granny Fantasies- Marilyn

Wife's Best Friend

Masturbation Confessions II

Sex with Vegetables

Female Masturbation Confessions- Kylie

Work Sexual Fantasies

Sexy Christmas Stories 2012

Mister Average's Best Erotica of 2012

The Pervert Priest

Public Sex Stories

The Inadequate Husband and the G-Spot.

Masturbating Author

1984 Erotica

An Inadequate Husband and the Twenty Year Old.

The Wife Swap

Older men, Younger women – The Phone.

Older men, Younger women – Sex Teacher

Older men, Younger women – The Dice